Night of
the Whale

Night of
the Whale

Jerry Spinelli

Little, Brown and Company
Boston / Toronto

First Edition

Library of Congress Cataloging in Publication Data

Spinelli, Jerry.
    Night of the whale.

    Summary: Six rowdy high school seniors staying at a beach house for
the summer are determined to devote themselves to partying until the
night they encounter a group of beached whales.
    [1. Whales — Fiction.   2. Wildlife rescue — Fiction]   I. Title.
PZ7.S75663Ni   1985   [Fic]   85-10119
ISBN 0-316-80718-4   7.00

BP

Published simultaneously in Canada
by Little, Brown & Company (Canada) Limited

Printed in the United States of America

Beth

Acknowledgments

With much gratitude for their help in filling in the blanks and untangling the knots, I thank the following contributors to this book: Barbara Pool, Irene Seipt, Harriet May Savitz, Michael Spinelli, Kevin James, Sue Vision, Betsy Hoffman, Ray Lincoln, Bob Sherwood, Carl Francis, Joseph Mesi, Dorian Olivera, Jane Tocci, Stephanie Owens Lurie, and Patricia Fiorelli.

If some thanks can be more special than others, they must go to Bob Schoelkopf and Sheila Dean and Bob Schoelkopf, Jr., all of the Marine Mammal Stranding Center, Brigantine, New Jersey; and, as always, to my wife and fellow author, Eileen.

J.S.

Night of
the Whale

The First Day

Oh God."

"Oh no, please no, *please*."

"This can't be happening."

"I'm going to spit."

The first fat raindrops flopped onto the windshield just as we were humping over the little drawbridge that leads into the heart of Ocean City.

"Look ahead. Over the ocean. Blue."

"Try looking back."

We all looked back. The sky was dirty socks as far as the eye could see.

Seventeen years you wait.

Lauren piped from the back: "Digger! This window doesn't close!"

Digger turned on the wipers. One of them worked — the one not in front of him. "So?" he said. "Think of it as a convertible."

Everyone but Lauren laughed. If there was anything to be queen of at Avon Oaks — Homecoming,

3

the May — Lauren was it, and that meant she was as much at home perched on a convertible as I was on a school bus. She growled for a good minute about getting wet, before Timmi, who was in the middle, sighed and traded seats with her.

Digger gunned it down Ninth Street, tooted as we passed a pink restaurant called the Chatterbox, hung a right at the last street before the Boardwalk, and soared up the length of Ocean City — past the Twenties, the Thirties, the Forties. People were coming up from the beach, some running, some lugging collapsible aluminum chairs. I thought about the wheelchair on the roof. Was it okay in the rain?

"The house is back on Thirty-second," Wags announced to the driver. As part of her graduation present, Wags's parents had said she could spend Senior Week at their house at the shore. She had been allowed to invite five friends.

"I got a date with the Atlantic Ocean," said Digger.

By now, the windshield wiper on Breeze's and my side wasn't doing so hot either; it was just taking an occasional drunken swipe at the rain.

Somewhere in the Fifties Digger hung a left and didn't stop till the car was nose to nose with a sand dune high as a house. I could hear the surf booming beyond. Digger popped out one door, Breeze the other.

Breeze cartwheeled over the dune and vanished, but Digger stayed on top long enough to spread-eagle against the cannon-smoke skies and bellow: "Freedom! Freedom! *Fur-reeeeedom!*" Then he was gone.

I leaned back and closed my eyes. I needed sleep bad, what with graduation the night before, and then the parties. Digger's front seat felt like a feather bed. I was dreaming of trying to pull my diploma from Mr. Cristofaro, the principal, who wouldn't let go of it, when I heard people howling and groaning in the back and Lauren going, "Now I *am* going to spit."

I opened my eyes. There was Digger (How did I instantly know it was him?), looming over the dune, stoop-shouldered and droopy-armed as an ape, and he was covered with seaweed. It hung like a green mop over his head; it draped over his shoulders and around his waist. It was not the bright, grassy, semi-slimey stuff that I had always pictured seaweed to be: some was olive-green and frilly, like romaine lettuce; the rest was knobby, like a necklace, and yellowish. It added up to grisly.

Digger showed none of his usual hysteria. He simply shambled down from the dune and into the car. Trapped in the front between him and Breeze, I made myself as narrow as possible, trying to stay dry.

For a while the car was perfectly silent, except for the faint rattle and pop and drip of the seaweed. I stiffened as an olive-green tentacle slid down my arm. There was a vague odor, not of garbage really, but of something just beginning to lose its grip on freshness.

"I want to go home," said Lauren.

With a plump, liquid rustling, The Thing from the Deep moved, the car started, and we were on our way.

The house on Thirty-second Street was a white bungalow with aqua trim and a ramp as well as steps leading up to the front door. Since the wheelchair was wet from riding on the roof, Timmi and I carried Wags directly into the house. I tried to play it cool, but having to hold one of Wags's lifeless legs in my hands made me a little shaky. We got her onto the sofa, me nearly dropping my half of her, and while I was wondering like a moron what to do next, Timmi was bringing in the chair, unfolding it, drying it off, and hauling Wags into it.

Wags poked me and winked. "Good job, Mouse."

The only belongings that qualified as "luggage" were those brought by me and the three girls. Digger had all his stuff in a gym bag. Breeze, naturally enough, had nothing.

I had to take Lauren's suitcase in, because she refused to leave the car. "Not as long as he's like that," she said.

Meanwhile, The Thing from the Deep took full advantage of the situation. It appeared hideously at one car window after another, finally dangling a knobby tentacle into the uncloseable window and drawing ear-piercing shrieks from Lauren. Curtains could be seen moving in windows across the street.

"Okay, Digger," Wags called from the front door, "out back. Shower stall. Metamorphose." She heaved him his gym bag.

I started checking out the house, but I got no farther than the first bedroom. I am cursed with smallness in many things (size, stomach capacity, et cetera), but there's nothing small about my appetite for sleep. My eyes were shut before I hit the pillow.

Next thing I knew, a cold, wet something was being inserted into my hand, and fingers were prying open my eyelids. Digger — this time in human clothing. "Let's go, Mouse. No sleeping allowed." The cold, wet thing was a can of beer.

I was led into the living room. Everybody was there, on the floor (except Wags). It was still raining.

"Are you a virgin?"

The question came from Breeze. Everyone was looking up at me, grinning. Two large pizzas sat in the middle of the floor.

"Let's not belabor the obvious," said Wags. "We're playing a game, Mouse. Take a drink." I took a drink. "Breeze, give him another question. Sit down, Mouse."

I sat down. A slice of pizza materialized in my other hand.

"Okay, Mouse," Breeze spoke again, "what's a Trojan?"

The pizza drooped until the tip touched my leg. With a great effort I lifted it, but a dollop of cheese stayed behind on my jeans. I stared at it.

"Want to pass, Mouse?" said Wags. "You're allowed one pass."

"Uh — no —" I said, trying to shake off sleep. "I

know it. Trojan. Uh, soldier of Troy. Fought the Greeks. Made a wooden horse."

Chuckles.

"No, wait — the *Greeks* made the horse."

Howls.

I picked the cheese from my pants. I wondered if it would stain.

"Okay, Mouse, your turn," said Wags. She explained how the game went. Each person got a chance to ask any other person a question. The target person could pass on the first question; if they also refused to answer the second question, they got a point. The person with the most total points would have to go to Planters Peanuts on the Boardwalk and goose Mister Peanut. There was only one requirement concerning the questions: they had to be personal. Oh shit, I thought, *those* Trojans.

The game was called Interview. Not surprising. Friendship wasn't the only thing bringing us together for Senior Week — we were also all members of *The Acorn,* our school newspaper.

Wags Hallewagen was editor-in-chief.

Timmi Romano was business manager. She probably worked more than anybody, most of the time in her No. 44 football jersey.

Lauren Parmentier was girls' correspondent. She was also the Beverly of "Beverly on Beauty."

Digger Binns had spent most of the year as associate editor (strictly honorary, to keep him out of the way). But then, when the staff photographer came down with mono in April, Wags — to everyone's shock — tossed Digger a Polaroid OneStep and appointed him to fill the vacancy.

There is nothing more dangerous than an ignoramus with a camera and a deadline. For two weeks the whole school trembled, wondering where the Mad Shutter would strike next. No one — student, teacher, principal, janitor — was safe. Anywhere. No one believed Wags would actually print the pictures, but she did, and to this day, all over Avon Oaks, people are still talking about and laughing over our farewell edition of *The Acorn*.

Breeze Brynofsky was contributing editor. He contributed a column called "Breezin' " whenever he felt like it. Once he breezed in with a column on patriotism; Wags sent it off to the Freedoms Foundation at Valley Forge, and it won a medal. (Much to the surprise of the American History teacher, who nevertheless flunked Breeze for the year since Breeze neglected to show up for the final.) In fact, Breeze had yet to feel the beat of "Pomp and Circumstance": he had fallen five-and-a-half credits short of graduating. Not that it bothered him. As for the medal, he couldn't even remember who he had given it to.

Me, I was reporter-at-large. My standing order from Wags was "Don't give me the big story, give me the little story." Which suited me fine.

I went for the easiest target. "Digger," I said, "what's your middle name?"

Heads swung. Salivating grins.

"You'll die, Umlau."

"Middle name, Digger."

"I pass."

Groans.

"Okay, different question. How do you spell your middle name?"

Breeze pounded the floor.

Digger drained his beer can. "I" — he belched — "pass."

Protests. Boos.

"You're taking a point?" said Wags.

Digger nodded.

Next it was Breeze's turn. He wasted no time. "Mouse, what's Digger's middle name?"

Maybe if it wasn't Senior Week, maybe if I had not had it in my power to bring joy to those expectant faces, maybe if I had looked at Digger . . . "Devon!" I cried, and quickly ducked under the beer can that came flying toward me. It bounced off the wall amid a chorus of echoes: "Devon? . . . *Devon?*"

Digger's Revenge wasn't long in coming. Poor Lauren was next to him, so she caught it first. A look of horror spread over her face, her eyes bulged, she grabbed her throat and bolted. Wags took a sniff. "God save us," she rasped, and with one good stroke backed herself into the dining room.

Before you could say "beer fart," Digger was alone in the middle of the living room floor, nonchalantly munching on pizza and snapping open another can. The girls were discovering what most guys had long since learned from bitter experience: Digger Binns was apparently born without a noise-making mechanism. Of his many titles, he was most feared as "The Silent Sphincter."

Waiting for the air to clear, I wandered through the house. I was so tired I was dragging along the walls. I *had* to sleep. I had to find a place where I would be *allowed* to sleep. I came to a door. I opened it. It was a closet.

"*Aha!*"

Doomsday roared in Digger's voice. I jerked awake and stuff came clattering down upon me. Serpentine things flexed over my body.

"Mouse, look!"

I looked. Sudden blinding flash; click; whir. Digger's camera.

His voice emanated from the star that glowed between his shoulders. "I knew you hadda be somewhere in this house, you little pissant." He hauled me to my feet. "Here." He put something in my hand — the picture, still black. He led me away. I kept bumping into things, stumbling, but his grip was tight on my arm.

We came to a stop. The air was beery.

"Found him in a closet," I heard him say.

Other voices floated by:

"Let him alone."

"Look, he's not even awake."

"Sadist."

A knuckle began rapping on my skull; it stopped when I opened my eyes. The picture was coming into focus. I had been attacked by vacuum cleaner accessories.

I started taking my bearings. The beer cans had multiplied — on the floor, chairs, coffee table, TV. Two more pizza boxes had appeared, plus a herd of Nacho bags. Crusts and Nacho fragments were everywhere. Timmi was kneeling at the sofa, scrubbing one of the cushions with Mr. Clean.

"Game over?" I yawned.

That brought snickers.

"The public *execution*," edited Wags, holding her Rolling Rock to her heart, "is over." She swiveled, showing the bumper sticker on the back of her chair: I BRAKE FOR WORMS. Swaying in her seat, she wheeled a zigzag path to the front door, flung it open, bellowed "*I hate this rain!*" and slammed the door shut.

Wags was wasted.

"You're vicious."

The words came from Lauren. She was sitting on the floor with her knees drawn up to her chin.

Digger looked around the room. "Who?"

"I knew you were always a clown. But I didn't know you could be vicious."

"Luscious Lauren is upset," Digger turned to me, "because she lost the game." He draped his arm around me and spoke just loud enough for her to hear. "I'll tell ya, Mouse, it was disgraceful. She passed on eight straight questions."

"You're a human vulture."

"Waddaya say, Mouse? Think she'll do it to Mister Peanut?"

"A jackal."

"Mouse — Mouse, all I was doing was asking some innocent questions about her and the Admiral." I was getting the picture. The "Admiral" was Lauren's boyfriend, a midshipman at Annapolis. He was supposed to show up in two days, Monday. "Look," Digger said, "judge for yourself. Question number eight was the easiest of all" — across the room Lauren was edging forward to her knees — "Question number eight was" — Digger reached into his pocket; Lauren was on her feet — "What would the Admiral say" — Digger's hand was out of his pocket; Lauren was hurtling across the room — "ifhesawthispicture?"

The photo flashed before my eyes; Lauren lunged; she missed the picture but grabbed a handful of me, stumbled, lurched, and crashed into me, her chin landing on my knee with a sound like a single hoof beat on a city street. She scrambled to her feet; her lip was bleeding. The photo was gone, tucked somewhere in Digger's clothes.

A single slice of pizza remained on the coffee table. In one roundhouse motion Lauren snatched it up and walloped Digger across the face with it, gooey side down. "Swine!" She then flung the slice against an abstract painting on the wall and ran off to her room.

"I don't see why she has to get all upset," Digger deadpanned. "She said she was just scratching. I believe her. Don't you, Mouse?"

Out came the photo. It showed Lauren Parmentier — Homecoming Queen, May Queen — with her finger up her nose. Of course, Lauren being Lauren, it was the little finger. Still, it was up there all the way to the first knuckle, and when you consider how long Lauren's fingernails are, well, that itch must have been on the underside of her brain.

"One piccher," declared Wags, forefinger in the air, "is worth a thousand boogies. Die, can!" She coiled and launched herself across the floor toward a Rolling Rock lying empty on its side, apparently intending to crush it with one of the big back wheels. She missed it altogether.

Timmi took her Mr. Clean over to the abstract painting.

Breeze opened the front door and threw up his arms. "It stopped!"

Lauren refused to come to the Boardwalk with us. She wouldn't even come out of her bedroom. Before we left, Digger put a match to the photo and slid it flaming under her door. As we left, we could hear her stomping out the fire.

We drove down Central to Fifteenth and parked. The ocean was two blocks away. I could hear it, but I couldn't see it; the Boardwalk, which sat like a platform above street and beach level, was in the way. My family usually goes to the Pocono Mountains for vacations, so I was pretty excited about seeing the Atlantic — until we went up the ramp to the Boards and I saw the girls and the food.

It was a feast for mouth and eyeballs. Chocolate-covered strawberries, girls from Bristol, ice cream waffles, girls from Central Bucks West, chocolate-covered pineapples, girls from Norristown, fudge, funnel cakes, chocolate-covered bananas. Seemed like you could get anything you wanted chocolate-covered except a girl.

Of all the places we hit, we didn't go into the one I wanted to see more than any other: the College Grille. Because of Digger. Ever since the previous summer I had been hearing about the College Grille. Check out the waitresses, they said. Finest in the East. Better than UCLA cheerleaders. But do you think we could get Digger to go in? He just kept walking, so we decided to leave it for another day.

Of course, there were swarms of guys on the Boardwalk too, and I was kind of sorry Lauren wasn't along. We could have shown her off. I must say, however, that in terms of showing off Avon Oaks pulchritude, we got pretty good mileage out of our fearless leader, Helene "Wags" Hallewagen. I don't think I realized, until I noticed the looks that other Senior Weekers were giving her (and *not* the wheelchair), just how much sex appeal she had left over from the days when her legs were strapped to skis or were kicking through the hundred-meter freestyle. She was sending the looks back too, and the words, slandering every guy unfortunate enough to be wearing the name of an alien school on his clothes. I swear, she had that Boardwalk in stitches and nearly every guy lusting after her.

There was one guy especially. He was making a big deal out of her sweatshirt, which said CORNELL (that's where she was heading in September). Seems he was attending Dartmouth. He thought he was the big dude — gonna impress the little freshman — but within seconds Wags had him flapping and dancing like a puppet, feeding him outrageous lies about herself ("My father is the majority stockholder of the Campbell Soup Company." "Next month I'm going to attempt to become the first female paraplegic to climb the Matterhorn.") He was panting, groveling, trying to line her up for football games and winter festivals through the year 2000. When she had him frothing at the mouth, she blithely tapped Timmi — "Onward, driver" — and blew him away like sand from her fingertip.

The sun went down, and that's when things started going bad.

First, somewhere near the Planters Peanut place, the salt air started to hit me like a bolt of chloroform. Mister Peanut reeled. It felt like my eyelids were dragging anchors. I tried to rally. I fought it with food — buttered popcorn, fresh-squeezed orange juice, chocolate-covered pretzels.

Then I noticed the chill, on my shoulders. My shoulders were bare because I was wearing a tank top. That's what Digger and Breeze were wearing. At first I dismissed it — a random gust from the ocean. But it wasn't a random gust; it was a continuous breeze and it was getting cooler by the minute. I thought: *This can't be. It's June. Nobody has jackets on.* But then I noticed — some people did have jackets on, and sweaters: old people, and babies in strollers. We checked into an open-front arcade, and a blast straight from the Arctic followed me in and nailed me by the air-hockey table. I studied Digger and Breeze pounding away at videos, but I couldn't spot a single goosebump on them. In fact, there was a gleam on Digger's shoulder that looked suspiciously like sweat.

A little later Breeze bummed four dollars from me, went into a food place, and came out carrying a paper cup as big as a bucket. It was called The Gallon, and it was filled to the brim with Breeze's favorite drink, Papaya Serenade. It was about then that I noticed the queasiness in my stomach.

By now we were almost to the end of the Boardwalk, at the amusement park. Digger dragged us over to the bumper cars, and while Wags held The Gallon, we clobbered each other around in our oversized toasters. When we staggered back out, we had a surprise waiting: Rantley was with Wags.

Eric Rantley has a nickname — Rocket — and it doesn't just stand for how hard he hits a tennis ball. It also refers to the way he treats people. It is said that his racquet has many notches, one for every girl he's aced.

Wags and Rantley had a relationship — if that's the right word — that didn't seem to make sense. He had been after her ever since tenth grade. He took out a million other girls, but Wags was the one he really wanted. As for Wags, she was never one to get super-serious about anyone; she saw a lot of guys. But to add a jerk like Rantley to her list, that was a shocker.

She went out with him during the first part of our junior year. Then came the accident. It was February. A busload of kids had gone up to Camelback for a ski weekend, Wags and Rantley among them. Wags didn't actually go *with* Rantley — she was with some girlfriends — but they were both good skiers, and Rantley was there, on the bus, on the slopes. The two of them were up on the Expert slope when it happened. Wags was hotdogging, trying a somersault. She didn't make it. Instead of on skis, she came down the slope on a stretcher. Broken back. Paralysis. Wheelchair.

To everyone's surprise, Rantley did not back off. If anything, he seemed to come on even stronger. It is said that he got his black Camaro just to impress Wags.

Digger bristled when he saw Rantley. Digger and Wags have been close ever since grade school. A sort of brother-sister act. More, maybe. When Digger was seven, his mother was killed pushing him out of the way of an oil delivery truck.

Digger and Rantley were jawing at each other across the wheelchair when Wags pushed Digger away and growled at us to go ride the Jackhammer, she could take care of herself. Rantley gave a lopsided grin. He was drinking from an orange-juice carton, but it wasn't orange juice you could smell on his breath from ten feet away.

By then I was fast losing my grip on good health. I climbed on the Jackhammer with the others, and when I came off I knew I had a ticket to Vomit City.

I groped through a gauntlet of tilting faces and carnival lights, and then I was away from the noise and lights, on a street, and that's when I gave Ocean City its first chocolate-covered gutter.

Along with sleeping, throwing up is one of the few things I do in a big way. I make an ungodly amount of noise, like I'm falling off a very tall building. When my stomach had given its all, I dragged my head up to find myself surrounded.

"Hey, Mouse, you okay?"

"He's sick, for God's sake."

"He's freezing."

"Damn, Mouse, look atcha."

"He's *blue*."

Something was put around my shoulders. I wrenched it off. It was Timmi's No. 11 jersey; it had been tied around her waist. I threw it at her. "I'm all right, okay? What do I look like? A baby?" I railed at their goosebumpless arms. "I'm a friggin' *graduate!*"

I shoved my way through them and headed back down the dark streets. Behind me I heard Wags's voice blending with the merry-go-round calliope: "No, let him go."

I was still cold and tired by the time I got to the house. And I was still sick, too, except that the sickness had moved up from my stomach to my heart. I was a disgrace. In two-and-a-half months I'd be a freshman at Dickinson College. What a joke. Where was I when they handed out appetites and stamina? I wanted to have a total college experience, but I didn't seem to have the tools. What would I do at a party — say, "Excuse me, it's eleven o'clock, I have to go to bed"? Or, "Do you have any smaller beer cans? This one's too big." I was supposedly going to college to study journalism, but if someone had handed me an application form right then, under Career Choice I would have put "Drinker of Gallons."

Lauren's door was still shut. No light beneath it. I put on pajamas and went to the bathroom and gave my teeth, and my whole cruddy mouth, a good scrubbing. One toothbrush — Lauren's probably — was dangling from the white porcelain fixture above the sink. I hesitated, dropped my brush in next to it, took it back out, and dropped it in one hole away.

On the way back to my room I nearly had a stroke — Lauren's door was open, just a couple inches. The hallway light barely penetrated the darkness of her room.

"Lauren?" I rasped. My heart was pounding.

"Mouse?" I relaxed — it was Lauren. The door opened a little more; her face appeared. Or I should say, her eyes — she was covering the rest with both hands. "I didn't know who it was."

"Yeah, just me," I said.

"Where're the others?"

"Oh, up on the Boards." I added quickly, "In fact, that's what I got — bored — y'know? What's the point in going up and down the same *Bored*-walk fifty times in one night? Who needs it?"

"So you're staying here?"

She had dropped one hand enough for me to see

that she was holding washcloth-wrapped ice cubes to her mouth. I could also make out the pink fringe of a shortie night-thing and a sliver of leg.

I shrugged. "I guess so."

She nodded — might have even smiled a pinch, I wasn't sure — and closed the door.

I heard her get into bed. I went to my room, took all the things out of my kit and lined them up on the dresser: toothpaste, comb, floss, Speed Stick, swabs, toothpicks, mouthwash, Clearasil, ballpoint pen, Band-Aids, Clorets, Coppertone, Noxema, lip ice. I read the directions on the Coppertone. I studied the ingredients in Noxema. No use — I had to go back, I couldn't let it rest there.

I stood at her door, my heart a basketball on a Sixers fast break. I tapped lightly on the door. Then louder. Springs creaked. Her voice was sleepy. "Who's that?"

"It's me. Mouse."

"You can't come in." Now her voice was keyed, wary.

I laughed. "Lauren, I'm not Digger. I just wanted to say I'm sorry my knee got in the way of your mouth. Okay?"

"Okay."

"And I'm sorry Digger gave you such a hard time. He's a real pain in the butt, y'know?"

"I know. Thanks."

"Okay, that's all. Good-night."

"Good-night."

As soon as I got to my room I started kicking

myself — I had forgotten to say the main thing I had intended to say.

Back at her door: "And Lauren, I forgot to tell you, for what it's worth, I actually never did see that picture. Digger took it away too fast . . . Okay?"

No answer.

"Okay, Lauren?"

"Good-night."

"Okay, just so you know now. G'night."

In my room, I turned out the light, flopped onto the bed by the window (Breeze and Digger could fight it out for the other bed), and discovered an incredible thing: I couldn't sleep! An even more incredible thing was beginning to sink in: *You, Warren "Mouse" Umlau, and Lauren Parmentier are going to bed in a house in Ocean City, New Jersey. Not a parent in sight. And your toothbrush is hanging with hers.*

I got up, turned on the light, pulled The List from my wallet, and read it:

1. Pull all-nighter (see sun rise)
2. Chug can of beer
3. Eat whole pizza (med. or lg.)
4. See a girl for first time and ask her out
5. Totally lose control
6. Hang around Acme frozen-food section wearing tank shirt for 1 hr. (simulates watching football game in Dec. in T-shirt)
7. Optional: moon someone

I added another:

8. Learn to vomit quieter

This was sort of my own personal orientation program for Dickinson. I had come down to the shore half expecting to knock off most if not all of the items before the week was over.

I added another:

9. Drink The Gallon

Before The List got any longer, I folded it, tucked it back in my wallet, and re-hit the sack.

I hoped the others wouldn't tell Lauren what a disgrace I'd been. I tried to picture the Admiral. It wasn't too hard, using the Naval Academy and Lauren herself as reference points. I knew that, being a midshipman and all, he probably didn't do most of the things on my list; but I also knew that if he wanted to, he could. And then I thought about Lauren standing darkly behind the door, and I remembered her saying, "So you're staying here?" It was hope that I had heard in her voice. Not that she wanted to mess around or anything like that, but she had been a little nervous: girl alone in house in strange city. She wanted someone else around, and she figured I was good enough for the job. *So you're staying here?* Because of my presence — me — she was sound asleep. *Rest easy, Admiral, I'm taking care of her.* It was the best I had felt all day.

The Second Day

Digger wore pumpkin-colored underpants, the kind they advertise in *Sports Illustrated*. He lay sprawled facedown on the other bed. Breeze wasn't in sight.

I hadn't slept in the same house with other kids since eighth grade, when my cousins from Michigan came to visit, and then everybody had been in pajamas. To this day my father wears pajamas, every night of the year, and so does my mother. And yet I knew, as soon as my eyes opened and landed on Digger, that pajamas were wrong.

As quietly and quickly as possible, I slipped out of my pajamas and headed for the dresser, and that's when I noticed the door — it was open. About a foot. Just enough for me to see Timmi turning into the bathroom. I froze, clutching my pajamas in front. Had she seen me? The bathroom door closed. I bolted for the door, slammed it shut.

I put on my usual white Fruit of the Loomies and

stuffed my pajamas — forever — into my dirty-laundry bag. Then I got out The List and made another addition:

10. Buy colored underwear

I remembered it was Sunday. Should I go to church? For the first time in my life I had to answer that question; it wouldn't be decided for me. Freedom.

The smell of bacon drifted into the room. As I finished dressing, I batted the church question back and forth. One thing was obvious: I didn't feel like going. But like homework and sex, church wasn't simply a matter of *Feel Like;* it was also a matter of *Ought.* And looking at it from the longest-range view I could manage — far beyond my mother saying as I walked out the door, "Don't forget church on Sunday" — I had no doubt that I *Ought* to go. But maybe there was another *ought,* with a lowercase "o," that said, You *ought* not always do what you *Ought* to do.

And there were environmental pressures. Ocean City is a hotbed of churchgoing. It advertises itself as "America's Greatest Family Resort," with the emphasis on *"Family."* That's why it's dry. That's why you have to cross the bay to Somers Point to get a beer.

A knock on the door . . . As I went to open it, the answer came sharp and clear, crystallized courtesy of my mother: I probably would have gone on my own, but you messed up my freedom of choice by telling me to. So the answer is no. You blew it, Mom.

It was Wags in a nightshirt, smiling, holding out

a glass of orange juice. "Welcome back to the world. Hungry?"

The smell of the bacon was glorious. I took the juice. "Lead on."

Wags spun about, folded her arms, and I pushed her into the kitchen.

Pushing Wags: it's one of many curious things about her that I notice but don't totally understand. I've always thought of wheelchair-bound people as being fiercely independent, wanting to show that, give them enough ramps and elevators, they can get around just fine without help from anybody. Not so, Wags. If she can help it, she almost never wheels herself anywhere.

Funny, because in nearly all other ways Wags Hallewagen is the most capable, strongest, most independent person — kid or otherwise — that I know. Maybe she figures she's entitled to being spoiled a little. Whatever, I'll say this — pushing Wags is more of an honor than a job. You discover this on the few occasions when Timmi, her chief chauffeur, is not around and you get handed the job. There is something about pushing a wheelchair that binds you to the person in it.

"Miss T. Romano," said Wags, "was kind enough to visit the local food mart and provide for us."

She swept her arm forward as we turned into the kitchen. Timmi and Lauren were at the stove, doing busy, earnest things to bacon and eggs. Lauren managed with one hand, while her other hand held an ice pack to her lip. The table looked like the cover of *Family Circle* — orange juice, matching mats and

napkins, silverware, cups and saucers, grapes, a
flower — and a sob-ball caught in my throat when I
counted the number of place settings: four. Obviously,
they had counted one of the guys in (still no sign of
Breeze), and the guy was me.

"Hi, Mouse." Timmi glanced over her shoulder.
"Scrambled? Sunny-side up?"

"Uh, scrambled," I answered. I was a little off-
balance. The pampering, the attention — it was more
like home than home. It was almost scary. Good-
scary.

I sat down. Lauren came around with coffee. She
said nothing and neither did I, and our eyes never
met, but the vapor that rose between us seemed to
whisper of something shared the night before. She
poured slowly and carefully, never spilling a drop.

Toast popped.

"Lauren, ready," called Timmi.

And so we had breakfast.

Afterward, Wags announced that we would all
accompany her to church. My first reaction was surprise. Wags? Who tips a can with the best of them?
Whose tongue has known the taste of the four-letter
word? Wags: church?

But on second thought, it wasn't surprising at all.
What comes off as hypocrisy in others shows up in
Wags as a kind of largeness, where everything and
everyone are welcome. Nothing seems to creak or
grate within her, so much room is there. I think one
of the biggest disappointments I could have in my

future years would be to learn that Wags had turned out to be a specialist.

Lauren balked.

Wags reached up, pulled the ice pack away.

"For God's sake, Lauren, you can't even tell."

"You can so," Lauren protested. "It's bulging out all over the place."

Of the two, Wags was more right — you could barely tell; and if you hadn't known, you probably would have thought Lauren was just wearing a sexy pout.

"Lauren," said Wags patiently, "number one, Paul isn't *coming* until *tomorrow*. Number two, when he *comes* he *won't* be able to *see* it. And number three, if he happens to *feel* it when he's *kissing* you, here" — she plucked a grape from the bunch in her lap and inserted it in Lauren's mouth — "*tell* him you're *sucking* on one of *these*."

Lauren laughed.

As we were heading out the door, Digger came running — "Mouse! Mouse!" — in his pumpkins.

Lauren continued on out the door. Timmi looked at Wags, at me, at her feet. Wags wolf-whistled.

"What?" I said.

"Gimme your watch. Hurry!"

He was doing an Indian war dance in front of us.

"What for?" I said.

He was pawing at me. "I'm goin' for the record."

"What record?"

"Just gimme —"

He snatched my wrist and practically tore my arm off trying to get my watch. Rather than risk having him break it, I let him take it. It's a digital with nine functions, including stopwatch.

He raced off, and moments later the silence was shattered — or should I say splattered — by the sound of water on water. It went on and on . . . Timmi tried to turn the chair to go, but Wags held the wheels . . . and on . . . Wags made fisty cheering motions . . . and on . . .

Only when the sound stopped did we leave. I closed the door on Digger's exultant yelps: "Sixty-three seconds! A new record! Sixty-three —"

On Sunday God rested, but not Digger.

We arrived home from church to find my pajamas draped over the horns of the white anchor that sat in the front yard. I was pretending not to know them when Wags took them off the anchor and handed them to me.

A minute later, inside, Lauren came screaming out of her room, anguish, then murder, in her eyes. She was clutching a large, framed picture of the Admiral that had apparently been propped in her room. The Admiral had a moustache, a missing front tooth, big ears, long hair, and something dribbling out of his nose.

Then, as Timmi was reaching for the Mr. Clean, another scream. Wags. Yelling rape. And then she was careening into the living room, dodging and ducking green missiles that pelted her and yelling, "Help! I'm being graped! I'm being graped!"

Despite all the havoc, the reason why we left so late for the beach was not Digger, but Lauren.

The rest of us — minus Breeze — were in the living room playing poker and waiting for Lauren to emerge from the bathroom. Digger was the first to get antsy; he hollered for her to hurry up.

Personally, the wait didn't bother me. For two reasons. In the first place, as I said before, I'm a mountain-vacation person, and I feel more comfortable in the glens and shadows of evergreens than on an open beach. It doesn't help that, physique-wise, I could never be mistaken for Conan the Barbarian, or that what little there is of me is so chalky white you might think I had stumbled into a convention of eraser-clappers.

Secondly, it seemed to me that there was something fitting about waiting for Lauren to make her appearance. I mean, *appearing* was the thing Lauren did best. She was a master. And isn't the main attraction the last to come onstage? There were no marquees, and nobody said a word, but a sense of it was in the air: the debut of Queen Lauren Parmentier in her new bathing suit would be a major Senior Week event.

Digger didn't quite see it that way. He finally popped up and went to the bathroom door. From my vantage point in the living room, this is what I saw and heard:

DIGGER [*pounding thunderously on bathroom door*]. Yo, Luscious! We don't have all summer! Let's go!

LAUREN. Digger! You want to blind me? I'm putting my eye shadow on!

DIGGER. You already had that stuff on!

LAUREN. That was this morning.

DIGGER. It takes an *hour?*

LAUREN. I've been in here five minutes.

DIGGER. You scrawny scallop! You're lying! Something's fishy in there! You gonna open this door or do I hafta —

LAUREN. Digger!

DIGGER [*pulling something from his pocket; appears to be a card, perhaps his driver's license*]. I'll huff 'n I'll puff!

LAUREN. Digger! I'm not *dressed!*

DIGGER [*working the card between door and frame, apparently trying to dislodge hook-and-eye lock*]. I'll snort 'n I'll sneeze!

LAUREN. Help!

DIGGER. I'll belch 'n I'll — [*tiny metallic sound of hook flipping out; Digger begins to push door open*]

LAUREN. Aaaaagh!

[*As the door slowly opens, there is a quick succession of sounds: clatter (cosmetics falling?), plop (eye shadow into toilet?), roll (lipstick across floor?), screeching scrape, repeated (shower curtain yanked open, then shut?)*]

DIGGER [*enters bathroom, out of sight; dead silence; then* . . .]. What's this?

LAUREN. What's what?

DIGGER. *This!*

LAUREN. Aaaaagh! [*shower curtain rustles*] Eyelash curler! Eyelash curler! Now get out! Leave!

DIGGER. We'll leave together.

LAUREN. I don't have my bathing suit. Just go, and I'll be out in a minute. *Honest.*

DIGGER. This it here on the towel rack? Purple?

LAUREN. Lavender.

DIGGER. Okay, here it comes. . . . Now I'm counting. One . . . two . . . three . . .

LAUREN. What are you *doing?*

DIGGER. You said a minute. In one minute, you know what happens to that curtain. . . . four . . . five . . .

LAUREN. No!

DIGGER. . . . eleven . . . twelve . . .

LAUREN. *Aaaaagh!*

DIGGER. . . . twenty-one . . . twenty-two . . .

Except for an occasional squeak, there were no more sounds from Lauren until Digger reached "Sixty!" — at which point Lauren let out a scream that didn't quit till every corpuscle in my body was standing at attention. What Lauren didn't know was that Digger was already leaving the bathroom as he stopped counting.

We resumed the poker game. We called our hands

and made our plays, but there was a tension below the card talk. I felt bad for Lauren; I thought Digger had gone too far. I sensed Timmi felt likewise. At the same time something bothered me about Wags. I had been a little surprised that she had not called Digger off, and now I was surprised to find her showing no signs of being fazed by anything other than the cards in her hand.

After a while came the faint rattle of the shower curtain opening, and then there were other small sounds, but we played quite a few hands and still Lauren did not appear.

At last Timmi got up. "I'm going to go see."

"Don't bother," said Wags, discarding. "Gimme three. She's okay."

Something resentful burned from Timmi's eyes down to Wags, who was intently arranging and studying her new cards. "Wags, I am not Digger. If I care to do something, I'll do it. I do not need your permission."

Silence.

Wags, whose eyes had never left her cards, extracted several from the fan and slapped them down smartly. "Three sixes."

When I turned back to Timmi, her eyes were gone from Wags and were fixed, unblinking, on Lauren, who was entering the room in a lavender two-piece and beach top, lavender sandals, lavender eye shadow, and of course her ever-present lavender shoulder bag.

I felt my throat tighten. The cards in Digger's

hand drooped for all to see. Lauren just stood there, composed, perfect, and I think that if that little cameo had lasted a second longer, three of us would have burst into applause.

As it was, Wags chirped, "Well, I guess three sixes wins. Let's hit the beach." She never once glanced at Lauren.

Unlike many Ocean City streets, Thirty-second leads directly onto the beach. No ramps or steps or barriers to deal with. The deep ruts in the sand tell the reason: Thirty-second Street is a point of entry for Beach Patrol vehicles.

When Timmi halted the wheelchair, I assumed we would each take a corner of the chair and haul it over the ruts. Digger had a different idea. He knelt before the chair, removed Wags's sandals, hoisted her over his shoulder, and galloped off; she whooped and smacked his rump like a jockey all the way across the beach until they both tumbled into the foaming sea.

The rest of us took it more slowly, setting up house on a pair of blankets. I was uneasy with all the sun, the exposure. I longed for a shadowy, pine-scented trail in the Poconos. It was ten minutes before I nudged off my moccasins, ten more for my shirt.

Timmi had no such fashion problems. She wore her No. 44 football jersey (it had been her brother's at Bucknell) over her bathing suit, and that's how she was every day at the beach.

I might have stayed longer on the blankets, but I saw something that made me very nervous — a hair, growing out of Lauren's chest, right where her cleavage began. To make matters worse, it was black. It curled back so that the tip of it nearly touched her. It even cast its own tiny shadow.

She lay in blissful ignorance beside me, gleaming with lotion, her eyelids covered by black plastic eyecups. She must have overlooked it in the bathroom, probably would have missed it in any light except in the merciless, dentist-chair brightness of the beach. And anyway, why would she even think to check? May Queens do not grow hair on their chests. Maybe God, as some sort of punishment, had planted it there just moments before.

Whatever, the mere thought of Digger catching sight of it gave me the shivers, and it wasn't long before my fears had pumped that hair up to the size of a tree trunk. I racked my brain for a diplomatic way to call it to her attention, but it was hopeless. I lathered myself with Coppertone, Sun Protection Factor 15 ("the ULTIMATE safeguard — 15 times your natural sun protection!") and took off for the sea, hoping God would see fit to remove it.

I was sloshing along the surf toward a jetty when I saw a familiar bouncing stride among the bodies ahead.

"Breeze!"

"Yo, Mouse. What's up?"

"You tell me. Where you been?"

"Fourteenth Street beach. You oughta see it."

"What do you mean?"

"Girls, man." He shook his head, remembering.
"Yeah?"
"Yeah."
"Lots, or excellence?"
"Both."
"All *right*."

"Picture" — he swept his hand across the horizon, wiping it clean — "the Pribilofs . . . five thousand seals . . . all identical . . . sunning themselves . . . on a single rock."

"Mercy."

He resumed walking.

"So," I said, "what're you doing *here?*"

He shrugged, which was as much answer as existed to the enigma that was Breeze Brynofsky. He could do that — plunge totally into something one minute, and walk away from it the next.

I bypassed one question (Where were his clothes? He wore only a bathing suit now) in favor of another: "So, last night. You didn't come back with the others?"

"Nah." He dashed ahead, sprang into the air, and somersaulted over a little kid pouring water into his sand-castle moat; he turned back, threw his arms into the air: "Tennessee!"

Tennessee. Avenue in Monopoly. Had he gone to Atlantic City? Curious as I was, I didn't want to interrogate him; so I just nodded and hoped he would decide to talk. After some more surf-strolling and aimless chitchatting, he did. He pointed across the bodies and blankets.

"That's the place."

"What place?"

"There."

"There *what?*"

He seemed to be pointing to some dunes behind the patio of a beachfront house.

"That's where Tennessee and Pennsylvania got together and preserved the Union." He put his hand over his heart. "Oughta be a marker there. 'On this site . . .' "

"You're making a lot of sense, Breeze." I tried not to sound too interested. Meanwhile, I memorized the landmarks that might guide me back to that spot. The beachfront house was squarish and had white siding, white wrought-iron patio furniture, and a huge, fringed yellow and white umbrella rising out of the patio table.

Breeze was now walking on his hands toward a particularly tiny castle-builder, who looked up in terror, bolted off into the water, then, seeing that was the wrong direction, reversed himself and ran back onto the beach, trampling his own castle along the way.

When Breeze finally righted himself, he again swept the horizon clean. "Picture: I'm walking back . . . dark, moonlight . . . somebody on the street, about a block ahead . . . a girl . . . she turns down toward the beach . . . I follow . . . come to the beach . . . nothing . . . surf, moonlight . . . I start walking . . . then . . . there she is . . . in a swale among the dunes

. . . tufts of beach grass, moonlight, sand — quiet and cool. No one says a word, only when I leave, she says, 'Don't you want to know my name?' I say, 'Okay,' and she says, 'Tennessee!' . . ."

He snapped his fingers and cartwheeled ahead. When he looked back, I was in the water.

"Come on," he called, "let's jog. See how far the beach goes."

"Not now." I waved, slogging through the breakers. "Gotta check out the water."

I didn't stop till I was safely waist-deep in the Atlantic Ocean. I had been getting the picture so clearly that the front of my bathing suit looked like an umbrella trying to open.

Now, concealed by the water, I mulled over the question: Was it true? With Breeze you could never be sure. Breeze's tales often seemed tall at first, but you couldn't dismiss them as easily as you would if they had come from someone else. His nonchalance gave his words as much credibility as doubt. If they were lies he told, he didn't cling to them. He didn't care if you believed him.

Maybe the answer was already protruding from me. Maybe truth was measurable in inches. I could feel the power: when I turned sideways the inrushing waves caught the billow of my bathing suit flush and swiveled me around to face the beach. So I kept myself pointed outward. A charter fishing boat moved lazily along the horizon. My feeling was that if I happened to lose my bathing suit, I would drill a hole through its hull. The boat was nearly out of sight by the time I left the water.

I wasn't sure what a "swale" was, but I guessed I was looking at one: a banana-split-dish-shaped depression that ran among the low-humped dunes behind the house with the white-and-yellow patio umbrella. The grassy tufts were there, trembling to an occasional puff from the sea.

There was no material evidence to be seen. The sand was a little disturbed, but no more than anywhere else. It was like trying to read a colonial-period tombstone; I couldn't make out the imprint of a finger or a heel, much less a whole body. But the longer I stayed there, the less proof I needed. My imagination began to re-create the scene as it might have been a mere twelve hours or so before — and within seconds I was ambling, then trotting, then dashing back into the concealing sea.

When I returned to the blankets, everybody was there but Breeze, and he came along in another minute. I couldn't believe he had already gone to the end of the beach; it appeared endless to me.

Breeze parked himself on somebody's towel, since there was no room left on the blankets. But Wags, who lay at the other end, would have none of that. "Move over, people," she said. "*The Acorn* staff that tries together, lies together." We all shifted to the right, and Breeze rolled aboard.

"You guys missed all the action."

Lauren spoke, elegant and inscrutable, from behind her black eyecups. She looked as timeless and perfect as a sculpture discovered in an Egyptian tomb. I tried to picture her withering away with the coming years, but I couldn't. Neither could I spy the renegade hair from my place one body away (Timmi was between us). Maybe I had imagined it.

"What action?" I said.

"Oh, the big fight."

"Yeah? Who?"

"Oh" — she flipped her hand toward Digger, who was applying lotion to the back of Wags's legs — "Mister Binns and Mister Rantley. I really didn't witness all the gory details."

"The idiots almost drowned me," said Wags.

Digger smacked her rump. "Hey — did I take care of him? Did I get rid of that measle? Did I protect your honor?"

"Vanquished him, huh, Dig?" I said.

Wags was smirking. "Vanquished, all right. He threw a dead horseshoe crab at him."

Timmi put down the Harlequin Romance she was reading. "Roll over," she told me. "You're gonna burn." And then her hand was smoothing lotion over my back and shoulders. The feel of it, especially when she reached the small of my back, returned me to a summer night years ago when my mother carefully spread Noxema over my sunburned skin.

Timmi was finishing my back when I heard Wags growl, "Digger, I have some very stubborn and faithful nerve endings left down there, and they're telling me that somebody's finger is slipping under my bathing suit and onto my behind."

"Just testing," said Digger. "Thought you might be faking it."

Timmi dangled the tube of lotion in front of me. "You do the legs."

I don't know exactly how long it lasted by the clock, but for a minuteless kind of while I had an experience, a sensation that I had never had before.

There we were —

Breeze   Me   Timmi   Lauren   Digger   Wags

— basking in our coconut oils, drowsing in the sun. It was so *nice*. And it wasn't the nothingness that it seemed to be; it was just that there was nothing *wrong*. It was all nice and warm and buttery. And thought-less — that was it. The experience simply soaked into me, entering through my pores and weaving through my body. And then my brain got to its feet, shook it-self like a wet dog, and announced, "All right, enough of this. Let's get some thinking done around here," and the experience fled like a butterfly through an open window.

A minute later, Wags's voice came over the blankets: "What's in the bag, Mouse?"

This is a little thing between Wags and me. She knows my brain is almost always running full tilt, and sometimes she just likes to reach in and pluck out whatever happens to be there. She thinks of my head as a grab bag, like the kind you find at flea markets marked "10 cents." You don't know what's inside until you buy and open it. For my part, whenever Wags asks, I always try to tell her exactly what I'm thinking at that moment.

And so I answered her: "Nuclear war."

Groans, moans, hisses.

"Thanks a lot, Mouse."

"You really know how to cheer things up, Mouse."

"Let's hear it for annihilation."

"Well," I said, "is anybody interested in hearing the *context?*" The only answer I got was a flying flip-flop that conked me on the head. "Okay, fine, forget it." I closed my eyes.

Wags's voice hurdled the bodies between us. "*I* want to hear the context."

"Okay" — I sat up, facing the sea — "the context is this: I was lying here thinking how great this all is. School over. Twelve years. I mean, look at that scene out there" — Wags alone bothered to look — "the ocean. Blue sky. Boats. People. Sails. Digger ought to take a picture of it and call it 'Paradise' — and I was just thinking I can't imagine, I can't even *imagine* a nuclear bomb wiping all this out. I'm looking out there now, and I'm trying to picture a colossal gray mushroom cloud taking up half the sky, and I can't."

"Mouse —" said Lauren, but I kept going, I was just getting warm.

"I can't believe that this spot right here — the Thirty-second Street beach at Ocean City, New Jersey — is factored into the microcircuitry of some missile in some silo in Outer Siberia. *Look* at that scene — look at *us*. How can you *be* here and believe it?"

"Mouse" — Lauren was holding her eyecups above her face — "that's e-*nough*."

"Go back to sleep, Lauren," said Wags, resting her head. "Nobody bombs during Senior Week."

As I lay back down, I heard Timmi, her face never straying from her Harlequin, say softly, as if to herself, "*I* believe it."

In less than five minutes I was on my feet, putting my mocs and shirt back on.

"Where you going?" Digger challenged. "You better not be sneaking off for a nappy-poo."

"Fourteenth Street beach," I called. "Ask Breeze if you want to know why."

I was a good Frisbee throw on my way when I heard a horrendous howl. I glanced back just long enough to see Lauren, her hands crossed over her chest as if in death's repose, and Digger standing above her, straddling her like a conquering warrior, holding aloft in his hand something too small for me to see at that distance.

It was a pretty good hike to the Boardwalk, which didn't begin until Twenty-third Street. I had to go well past Fourteenth before I found what I was looking for — not in a men's store, but in a gift and novelty shop, in the back, in lurid purple lighting on a shelf beneath a poster of a naked three hundred-pound woman with a rose in her teeth: men's bikini briefs. I bought three. Mano Black, Midnight Blue, and Chianti.

Then I went under the Boards, lay down my towel in the cool shade, and sacked out for a while. The seaside sun can really take it out of you.

I went with the Midnight Blues.

They felt funny at first, as though they were falling down, even with my jeans on over them. I kept trying to pull them up higher, but no matter how hard I pulled, the waistband wouldn't clear the tops of my hip bones.

I stayed in the bedroom for a while, trying to get the feel of them. It was hard to believe girls could be comfortable walking onto a beach, wearing something like that, and *no* jeans on over them.

I was amazed at the effect underwear could have on a person — one's own underwear, that is. Questions that I had had about the world of female underthings — why colors? why lace? why style? who cares? who sees? — began to inch toward answers. There was a whole psychology at work here that I had been missing, something to do with the Under and how it might be reflected by the Outer.

And, in fact, as I ambled around the beds and struck some male model–type poses (keeping a sharp eye on the closed door), I did start to feel a little different, a little more sure of myself, a little less funny, a little more sexy. I rooted through Digger's gym bag for cologne or after-shave but couldn't find any.

I opened the door as though it were a test booklet. Had I really changed? Would it show?

I walked past the bathroom, where Lauren was scooping upwards at her eyelashes. An eyeball shifted in my direction. Had she sensed it?

Wags and Timmi were in the living room. "You're starting to take as long as Lauren" was Timmi's greeting. She was still deep in her Harlequin.

I went to the front window. Digger was sitting on the hood of his car, waiting to drive us to the Boardwalk. Breeze was gone again.

When I turned around I found Wags looking at me, up and down. Her eye had caught something, sensed something (my aura?). She was hesitating, as if double-checking herself, as if considering what to say. My Midnight Blues were smoldering.

And then she said it: "Uh, Mouse, I don't want to sound like a mother, but maybe you ought to bring a jacket along. Remember last night."

By the time we reached the Boardwalk I was gladder than ever about what I was — and wasn't — wearing (no jacket), because we were heading for the College Grille. Even the girls wanted to go; they wanted to see the legendary waitresses for themselves. Up on the Boardwalk, we picked up Breeze and dropped Digger, who still didn't want to go in.

The waitresses were everything they were rumored to be. As we headed for a booth, Breeze and I kept poking each other:

"Lookit there."

"Check this one."

"*That* one."

"*Behind* you."

It was more than just their looks that got to me; it was also knowing that they had come from campuses all over the East. They had already been where I was going. In their slightest gestures and movements I read intimations of woolen scarves and football weekends, strolls across moonlit quads, trysts high in library stacks. These were not mere girls — these were *college women*. Beautiful. Sharp. Experienced. They could probably spot a white Fruit of the Loomie a mile away.

The whole place in fact reeked of college. Pennants on the walls. Football-player types. "Oral Exam" instead of "Menu."

After deciding on a Purdueburger, my main concern was thinking up a question to ask our waitress. By the time she came with the drinks, I had the question but I lost my nerve. I concentrated on my Midnight Blues, and when she arrived with the food, I was ready.

"Any of you here happen to go to Dickinson?" I said.

"Don't think so," she said, coolly dealing the rest of the burgers.

I was busy inspecting my Purdueburger and feeling grateful that the waitress had condescended to answer me, when she laid the catsup on the table and lit up my whole tree: "Is that where you go?"

"Uh, yeah," I said.

She nodded, picked up her tray and was gone.

"So you *go* to Dickinson, huh?" drawled Wags, searching for the best point of attack on her Pittsburger. "And how *are* things at good ol' Dickinson, anyway?"

I took another five minutes of flak, but I didn't care. I felt that the waitress-goddess's words had anointed me. I had a piece of paper at home that said I had been accepted into Dickinson. Now I was accepted into *college*.

Outside, the shadows were marching across the Boards. Digger wasn't around, so we cruised on without him. When the others checked into an arcade, I stayed out and sat on a bench by the beach-side rail, where it was sunny and warmer.

A sign said no one was allowed on the beach after 10 P.M., but most of the mob had already left with the falling sun. The few who remained seemed to truly belong there, people who found the seashore more than a flat, treeless place to serve as a griddle for toasting skin. There were a couple of surfboarders; two hand-holding, shoe-carrying lovers; a shell-gatherer; a straight-standing, hands-in-pockets sea-gazer; and a grizzled old coot sweeping the trampled sands with a metal detector.

I was gazing at the sea and the sea-gazing man when I heard — or thought I heard — a tiny voice bleating, "Help." The shadow of the arcade roof had reached my feet; a chill went through me.

Then again, the voice — "Help me, please" — so tiny, as if an insect had spoken.

Under the Boardwalk?

I started looking around, and then I saw it, on

the Boards just a few feet away, at one end of the bench: the charred, foot-long "corpse" of a doll. (From the boots and an unburned portion of camouflage pant leg, I guessed it was G.I. Joe.) It was lying on its back, and it was being maneuvered somehow through the crack between the Boardwalk planks.

It moved. "Please, somebody, help me. The pain is unbearable . . ."

"Digger," I called down, "you're really a sicko, you know that?"

The head rose slowly — a black, fire-roasted potato — and looked at me. "Please . . . please . . ."

The head turned, and I saw that other people were beginning to notice. Most of them slowed down and continued to walk, looking back. A little kid wanted to stop, but his mother dragged him on; he started to howl. A pair of junior-high girls stopped and stayed about ten feet away, holding their mouths as though waiting for the signal to laugh. A stooped old man in white shoes halted, then shuffled closer till he was looking straight down at it.

I was sitting at attention in the middle of the bench, not sure what to do. The old man kept staring down as the tiny voice went on: "Please . . . somebody . . . the pain . . ." At one point he touched it, ever so lightly, with the tip of one of his white shoes.

Then Wags was charging across the Boards. She wheeled right up to the thing, said "Excuse me" to the old man, reached down and swiped the thing off the Boardwalk and onto the sand below. Jutting up through the crack was a pointed stick, the kind you're left with after finishing a frozen banana.

Slowly, as though surrendering to the fury in Wags's eyes, the stick descended till it was gone. A few seconds later Digger mounted the steps to the Boardwalk, suavely flipping the stick over his shoulder. The junior-high girls giggled. Someone applauded.

Wags rolled over to Digger, pushed herself up wobbling on one hand, and slapped him with a roundhouse right.

"Hey," came a voice from the onlookers, but no one moved. Digger was looking up at the sky, his teeth clenched, one side of his face bright red.

Then something — a gasp from the crowd — swung my attention back to Wags. Everyone was staring at her, alarmed — even Digger — but I couldn't tell why because I was directly behind her chair. Then Timmi burst through and knelt before the chair; I got up and came around and saw what the matter was. One of Wags's legs was rising, bent at the knee and rising to her chin; and she was trying to push it down, her eyes squeezed shut, trying to make it go down.

By the time we got Wags to the car, the leg had pretty much returned to normal. "Sorry, gang," she said. "Sometimes they spasm." She lay on her back in the back seat, with her legs resting on my lap and Timmi kneeling on the floor massaging them.

Wags winked at me. "Here's your chance, Mouse. Take a leg."

So I took a leg and followed Timmi's example, kneading the soft muscles from thigh to calf.

Wags called to Digger: "Jeeves, head for the Point. We need some brew."

Back at the house, the evening's festivities kicked off with a beer-chugging contest. Only three entered the competition: Mr. Digger Binns, Miss Wags Hallewagen, and a last-minute entry bowing to popular demand, me. The other two ladies, Miss Romano and Miss Parmentier, sent their regrets. Mr. Brynofsky contented himself with two quart bottles of Papaya Serenade.

Breeze was timer, with my watch. Digger was timed in 5.67 seconds, Wags in 6.25. I came in at 15 seconds, but that turned out to be unofficial, since I had drunk only half the can.

Under international rules, I was given a minute to resume. It seemed hopeless; I swore half the Atlantic Ocean was in my stomach. Then, with Breeze calling down the seconds, a belch erupted out of me and didn't peter out till my knees were weak and my stomach empty. I snatched the can and to a chorus of cheers polished off the rest in 8 seconds flat, making a total chug time of 23 seconds. Then, for good measure, I crushed the can.

The fans went crazy. Digger and Breeze rode me around the room on their shoulders. I wasn't kidding myself — I knew I had a long way to go to be truly a Drinker of Gallons — but I felt also that I had turned the corner, and surprisingly, it was not so much the chug that impressed me as the titanic belch, which I never would have thought I had in me. I rode those shoulders into the dawn of a new outlook, and by the time I stepped back down to the floor I had drained another half a can.

"A little while longer, and we'll be ready for a piss-off," announced Digger. "You in, Wags? How about you, Luscious?"

The girls said some other time. Wags suggested that as a substitute we all tell our favorite "tinkle" stories.

So the stories came out and the beer went down. It was all very nostalgic, since the best tinkle stories tend to take place when you're little, so we wound up reliving our grade-school days.

Wags came last. She told her story, and then she said that as a treat she would give us a "bonus point of interest." So she told us about foxes, and how when they take a leak they're doing more than just taking a leak. "Actually, they're staking out their territory," she said, "squirting a little here, trotting on, stopping, squirting, and so on, laying down scent — an invisible fence — that keeps other foxes away."

I don't know why, but that tickled me more than anything I had heard in years. I kept picturing these little red foxes trotting around with surveyor's tripods over their shoulders. I couldn't stop laughing.

My memory starts to get a little muddled at that point. The two things I remember most clearly are grappling with the problem of how to gracefully exit myself from the house so I could search for Tennessee, and the swelling and hardening of my bladder, as though someone were pumping it up.

"Let's piss-off," Digger kept pestering, but I was holding out; I, not Digger, would break the world record, if I had to drown from the inside-out trying.

Then we were talking about coed dorms, and somebody said the bathrooms were coed too, and what would you do if you went into a stall and sat down and saw a pair of fancy lace panties hanging over the ankles next to you? And what would you wear through the hallways and in the lavatories? Just how "decent" would you have to be?

And it all swirls together then: Midnight Blues and bloated bladders and a loud gong gonging and whistles and finally puncturing my bladder — a blessed Mississippi of piss — only to look down and see beside me, standing on two legs, taking his own little leak, winking up at me, the cutest little red fox . . . and out there, in the dunes, in the swale, waiting, Tennessee, in the star-fallen sands by the surf that goes round and round, waiting, waiting . . .

And then someone was shaking my shoulder and calling my name, and I was in bed waking up.

The Third Day

Mouse, come on, get dressed."

It was Wags. It was dark.

As I tried to get up, I made a startling discovery: my bladder had somehow shifted from my abdomon up to the place where my head used to be, and sat there now like a giant beach ball. I did not so much get dressed as allow Wags to dress me. I cooperated as much as I could, lifting arms and legs to her commands, but I concentrated mostly on the beach ball, which was threatening to roll off if I did not give it total attention.

Somewhere in there it came to me that I was having a hangover. My first. I could understand now why they were such unwelcome things, and yet I couldn't help feeling a little pinch of pride.

"Here, drink," I heard her say, and the warm rim advanced to my lower lip.

It tasted terrible. Bitter.

"Black coffee," she said. "C'mon, more."

Beach-ball-headed as I was, I dimly resented Wags trying to banish my hangover so quickly. I wanted to savor it just a little while longer, truly experience it.

The cup went away.

"Okay, here, sit down."

I was moving, cruising. It was nice.

"Okay, end of the line, off."

I opened my eyes, got up, and only then realized that I had ridden Wags's lap from my room to the front door.

"Now listen, Mouse. Hold on to my chair while I go down the ramp here. You're going to push me up to the beach, and by the time we get there you're going to be awake and functional, understand?"

I did as I was told, but I didn't understand. Why was she getting me up in the middle of the night to go to the beach? Was she looking for Tennessee too?

Maybe it was Wags's power of suggestion, or the salt air — I don't know — but by the time we reached the beach, my head was starting to feel a little more like a head, and I was awake enough to notice that she had put a jacket on me.

Wags pointed. "Look."

The sea and the sky appeared to be nearly the same color and substance, as though they had merged while Ocean City slept. What we were witnessing was the coming apart, and the line of separation was the light across the horizon, soft as the TV glow that shows beneath a closed door. It wasn't night after all. It was morning. And it was all new — endless pastures of beach and sea and sky. For the first time I felt the full impact of being on the pulverized edge of the continent, so finely feathered it seemed one full-weight step upon it could tilt North America into the Atlantic.

"Down to the wet sand," said Wags. "I'll try to help."

It was murder, getting that chair through the soft sand. By the time we hit the damp, firmer sand, we were both slumping.

"Okay," she gasped, "that way, to the jetty. Hurry!"

I hurried. I still didn't know what was going on, but whatever it was I was getting caught up in it.

The extent of the high tide was marked by the line of debris that had been deposited, a kind of humped horizon of shells and driftwood and seaweed and crab pieces and trash, a motley collection of unwilling Columbuses. I got the impression that during the night the sea had swabbed its own deck clean, and the clumps of seaweed were the mops it had left behind. A spindle-legged bird sprinted ahead, daring us to race. Gulls carouseled above.

By the time we reached the jetty, the eastern sky looked as though it had been brushed every color in Lauren's bag of cosmetics. Wags had me park her alongside a jetty rock. It came up to her shoulder.

"Okay, good enough."

She reached behind, took my hand, and led me around and down to a crouch in front of her. She took both my hands and held them gently in her own. For a while she just looked into my eyes and said nothing, not with words anyway.

"Mouse . . ."

She said my name, then was silent again.

"Mouse . . . I can't . . . do . . . everything I used to do . . ." My throat was thickening. "At least, not the *way* I used to do things. Sometimes now I have to find new ways to do the things I always wanted to do. Okay so far?"

I cleared my throat, nodded.

"Well" — she looked beyond me — "one of the things I always wanted to do was see the sun rise at the shore. And" — she smiled — "here we are."

"Yeah," I rasped.

She turned back down to me. "But that's not all of it. I also wanted to walk out to the end of a jetty, as far as I could go, and see what it's like. Something tells me sunrise is the best time to do it."

I started to get up. "Well, let's give it a try."

She burst out laughing and pulled me down. "God, Mouse, you're sweet. You're ready to start lugging me out there, aren't you?"

"Isn't that what you're saying?"

She grabbed my face in her hands and pulled me to her and kissed me. "No, goofball, not exactly. Those rocks are slick and treacherous. You'd kill us both."

"So then, what?"

"So. What I want is for you to do it *for* me. Or let's say, for me to do it *through* you." She smiled at the total bewilderment on my face. "Mouse — do you believe there's more than meets the eye? That stories happen that can't be reported in a newspaper, not even in Breeze's column, because there are no words for them? That we're all connected somehow? That something flows through us all like a stream, and that a leaf floating through one person can also pass through a second person, as long as the second person is downstream?"

I kept nodding.

She reached down to the sand and came up with a crab claw. It was blue and gray and orange-tipped, as though spray painted by the dawn. It was beautiful, really, just by itself, something you'd want to save, mount.

"See these things all over? You notice it's all you ever see? You never see a whole crab. Only sad, sorry pieces, all over the beach. Fragments of what they used to be."

"Pretty, though," I said.

She nodded, smiled. "Yeah, but not as good as a whole crab." She tossed the claw away; her eyes stayed where it landed. "Sometimes . . . I think maybe we're like that . . . fragments . . . not as whole as we think we are. You, me . . . we're pieces. Sections. Strewn across the beaches. A claw here, an eyeball there. If we could only find a way to put ourselves back together, find out what we add up to, what we once were."

Her eyes darted to the horizon, to me. "Mouse, it's almost time. Will you do it? Go out there? For me?"

I stood. "Okay, but I'm not sure I know what to do."

"Just get the story, Mouse. Just be yourself, that's

all. Be Mouse." I started to go. "Wait" — she grabbed
my arm, pulled me close. She put her hand under
my shirt and slid it up to the middle of my chest, over
my heart. She let it rest there for a few seconds and
peered intently into my eyes; reflected in hers I saw
all the dawn I would ever need to see. "Okay," she
smiled, "go."

I climbed onto the first rock and headed out. "Be
careful!" she called.

I understood now why she had laughed. The jetty
was hardly made for a person to lug himself across it,
much less someone piggyback. The massive, black,
blockish boulders seemed to be there as much by accident as by design, the dumped, ancient leftovers of
a pyramid-builder. I had to straddle chasms, drop down
to one rock, grapple up to the next.

After some twenty feet or so, the jetty left the
land. Now there was only water on both sides, and it
struck with a ferocity that made me flinch. It seemed
intent on punishing the jetty for its impudent intru-
sion. It slammed into the rocks with a dull, powerful
whmmp, like a collision of bull mattresses, then ex-
ploded upward and forward, slinging a patter of raindrops across the rocktops and flooding the flumes
between. It was relentless: even as one broadside hit,
the spent fury of the last was trickling down the cracks
and back out to sea.

By the time I got halfway out, I was soaked. I
looked back. Wags was facing me, her eyes closed,
one hand on a rock.

Compared to what lay ahead, the first half was a

cakewalk. I was beyond the low-tide line now, where rocks never had a chance to dry out. To make matters slipperier, green scum coated many of the surfaces. Colonies of barnacles and mussels lurked in the crevices.

It was scary. Toward the end, the jetty began to narrow and the sea raged and gnashed at me like a thousand lions. I went as far as I could, to the last rock that did not actually go underwater with every wave. I was shaking from the cold and wet.

Suddenly I remembered: the sun! I looked up, just in time. The crest appeared crisp and sharp as an orange; then it seemed to swell and melt, dripping, then spilling over the edge of the sea, like molasses over a countertop. And the sea became an accompanying orchestra: thrum of strings, blare of horns, boom of kettle drums, thunderous clash of cymbals. I felt like applauding. What a performance!

If I had been strictly on my own, I probably would have gone back then. After all, what could top that? But I stayed, knowing Wags would have. I lowered myself carefully to all fours, the better to lodge myself against the flogging waves, clinging like a barnacle; and as I clutched my rock I seemed to lose something of myself, and of the world I lived in, as though my topsoil were being washed away. I began to feel less alien, more at home, on the black wet rock. And the sun that I saw emerging beyond the leaping wave spray seemed to be dawning on a day much earlier than the one I had awakened in. I trembled, but not from the wet or cold, for I began to sense something beyond the incredible. Wags was right — there are stories no words can tell; all they can do is swipe clumsily, like Digger's windshield wipers, at an insight or event.

Something hit me in the face. I looked down. It was a crab claw. I picked it up and put it in my pocket. The sun was well clear of the horizon. I got achingly to my feet and started back.

My sneakers squooshed at every step. My drenched hair flopped like seaweed over my head. I wiped water from my face and peered through the sea plumes down the avenue of rocks to where Wags waited, her arms thrust out to me. By the time I reached the dry rocks, I could see the tears streaming down her face. I ran the rest of the way and nearly bowled her over. We clutched and hugged and clung to each other. A pair of sniffled thank-yous were the only words.

A Frisbee came flying at me the moment we entered the house. Instinctively I caught it. It wasn't a Frisbee — it was a pancake.

Digger applauded. "Way to snag 'em, Mouse Dropping!"

"Wags —" Timmi whined from the stove, brandishing a spatula, "will you make him *stop*. You should've seen what he and Breeze were doing with the pancakes. Lauren and I are *trying* to *eat*."

Wags rolled her eyes and sighed to me. "What are we to do, dear? We just can't seem to leave the house for a minute without them tearing it apart."

I closed the front door. "I guess we'll have to send them all to boarding school, dear."

Digger snatched the pancake from me and took a bite. "So where were you two, anyway?"

"Oh, getting off by ourselves," Wags replied blithely and rolled away.

Digger stood there grinning at me and wagging his head. He held out his hand. "Mouse, congratulations."

I let him shake my hand, warily. "What for?"

He put his arm around me. "Last night, ol' dude."

"Well," I said, "not bad for a rookie, I guess. Twenty-three seconds. Not exactly in your league, though."

"*My* league? Shoot, you passed my league last night. You left my ass in the dust, man."

Then they were all turning to me, grinning, chuckling. My eyes met Timmi's; she turned back to her pancakes. Her face was red.

Digger grabbed a chair and sat me down. He crouched in front of me, a look of amused disbelief on his face. "You don't remember last night?"

"Sure," I said. "You and Breeze carried me around on your shoulders. How could I ever forget such a high honor?"

"Yeah, what else?"

"Stories, everybody told."

"Yeah, what else?"

I shrugged. "We talked. Coed dorms and all."

"*Talked?*"

"Yeah."

Digger looked at the others; another round of chuckles broke out.

"Right," he said, "you talked all right, Mouse ol' dude, loud and clear, but not with your mouth."

"What do you mean?" I said. My face was getting warm.

"You don't remember putting on a little fashion show? All dressed up in nothing but your new blue pantaloons? Showing the audience how you were gonna *ster-rolll* down the hallways in the coed dorms?"

"I remember talking."

Timmi had her eyes glued to the skillet. Lauren was studying her empty orange-juice glass. My face was boiling.

"Or how you decided to give us all a real treat and changed into your new *red* pair and modeled *them* for us?"

I looked to Wags. She nodded solemnly and whispered, "Spiffy."

"He's right?"

"For once."

I turned back to Digger. "I sort of remember whistles, and like, a gong."

Pandemonium. Timmi burnt her finger and ran to the sink.

Digger was doubled up on the floor. He looked exactly as he would have if he had been kicked in the groin, even down to the agony on his face and the tears in his eyes and the shrill, breathless gasping. "The g—, the g—" — at last he managed to speak — "the gong was that there frying pan. Breeze was beating it with a spoon and we were doing the whistling and you were bumping and grinding like a champ so hard we thought you were gonna throw your hips outta joint, oh God —" He went back into his kicked-balls routine. "Bree—, Bree—, you tell'm . . . th'rest . . ."

There was *more?*

"Picture this," said Breeze, wiping the "slate." "You just modeled your red drawers, and now you have to take a wicked whizz. Beer's coming out of your ears. So you go to the front door — here — open it up, go outside, still in your red drawers —"

"It was the bathroom," I said.

Another uproar.

"No, Mouse, sorry — you go out *this* door" — he opened it — "and you go down the ramp and walk about halfway to the sidewalk. You with me? You stand there for a while, looking at the anchor, and then you walk over to it and you take your whizz."

"Jesus "

He held up his hand. "But wait, that's not all. So you're taking your whizz —"

Digger rolled over and yanked on my ankle. "Mouse, unbelievable whizz, really. It's a crime nobody had a watch on it. Go ahead, Breeze."

"So — you're standing there with this whizz that won't quit, but what you don't know is that ten feet away a cop car has pulled up to the curb and the cop is just sitting there watching you. So by this time Digger and I are out there to haul you in, and the cop waits till you're finished and he says, 'Uh, pardon me, there,' and you look up and stare at him for a while

and say, 'Yes, sir,' and he says, 'Front yard's no place
to be taking a leak, son,' and you say, 'I'm not takin'
a leak, off'cer, I'm stakin' out my terr'tory.' "

It was five minutes before the house stopped rock-
ing. I just sat there on my chair in the middle of the
living room, and from the fuss that Digger and Breeze
were making over me, the chair came to have more
and more the feel of a throne. In a way, I guess I had
wished for a coronation like this, but now that it
was happening I couldn't seem to decide how I felt
about it. I wondered why Wags hadn't mentioned it
earlier.

Not long after the last chuckle faded, the doorbell
rang. Digger anwered it. I heard a voice say "Helene
Hallewagen." When Digger turned around, he was
holding a long white box with a wide red ribbon. He
dumped it onto Wags's lap and went back to the bedroom. Wags opened the box. It was long-stemmed
roses. A dozen. She looked at the card.

"Rantley," she said.

This being the day the Admiral was due to come
calling, Lauren stayed behind as we headed for the
beach. Along the way Digger kept cutting up Rantley.
Rantley this, Rantley that. The more Wags seemed
not to hear, the nastier Digger got.

Finally, as the rest of us were lifting Wags like
an aluminum-enthroned Cleopatra over the tire ruts,
he snarled, "So, maybe you'll get the honor of being
the next notch on the Rocket Racquet."

Wags waited till we set her down, then turned

haughtily to him. "My deah, I have *alrrready* been informed that *I* shall be worth *thrrrree* notches."

While the rest of us were cracking up, Digger propelled her through the soft sand as though it were asphalt; he didn't stop at the surf, but slogged on until at last he tipped the chair forward and literally dumped Wags into the ocean. She proceeded to swim calmly out beyond the breakers to smoother waters.

It was more than a different beach — it was a different world from the one Wags and I had shared only hours before. The jetty, several blocks away, seemed nothing more than a mundane seashore prop, a stubble on the continent's chin. Children darted in and out of its crannies. One of the black rocks, tilted conveniently toward the noonday sun, had become a tanning tray for someone on a brilliant pink towel.

Gone were the birds that ran and the clamshell odor. Neither the air nor the sand — both warm now — retained the faintest pulse of the awesome and tumultuous Creation I had witnessed. And behold, in six hours the human race had multiplied and were dwelling on a million blankets, and the people dreamed a million dreams (for the blankets were magical), and the music from a million radios transported them as far as they wished to go, and none of them dreamed how close they were to the wet black rock at the end of the world.

I dozed off then, reclimbing the tree that Wags had shaken me down from in the morning dark. When I awoke, I found myself under a towel from shoulders to ankles.

"You'd've gotten burnt to a cinder," said Timmi, turning a page in her Harlequin. "You didn't even put any lotion on."

"Did you?" I said. I felt my skin.

"God," she whined, "what do I look like, your *mother?*"

I sat up to put some SPF 15 on and discovered that Lauren was with us. She was doing her toenails. The toes were separated by pieces of rolled-up paper. Her blanket section looked like the cosmetics counter at Wanamaker's. "I'm not waiting there all day," she shrugged, "midshipman or not. Let him find me."

I noticed the wheelchair was gone.

"Where's Wags?"

"Rantley," said Timmi. "Took her for a stroll." She sneered the last word.

I had to admit, it was hard for me to side with Wags on the Rantley issue. I couldn't think of anyone who really liked him; and while Wags wasn't actually going out with him, she did know about the notched racquet and what a wipe he was, and why someone of her caliber didn't just slam the door on him was more than I could figure.

I dozed off again. Still feeling the aftereffects of all that beer. I was dimly aware of a towel slipping over me.

When I awoke again it was time to go. Wags was back, minus Rantley, and everybody (except Breeze, who had long since vanished) was waiting for Lauren's last toenail to dry.

Wags spun a Frisbee at me. "You always go wild like this when you hit the beach, Mouse?"

Digger fetched my moccasins, slid them onto my feet, and helped me up. He was beaming with brotherhood. "Don't listen to her, Rat. You get all the shut-eye you want."

"Huh?" I said. "What's this 'Rat'?"

"You, man. Mouse don't fit no more." He brushed some sand from my arm. "Yeah, Rat's gotta recharge, 'cause him and me's gonna blow it out again tooo-night!"

At Wags's suggestion, Lauren taped a note for the Admiral on the front door, in case he showed up while we were gone.

Once again Digger balked at going to the College Grille, but we told him this time he had no choice; we weren't about to leave him outside and risk another dying-doll episode. He begged enough time to run into a drugstore. When he came out he had a five-pack of cigars. Phillies Panatellas.

He held one out to me. "Rat?"

I took it. I was kind of afraid not to. I put it in my shirt pocket.

Going into the College Grille the second time was even better than the first. I wasn't just an awestruck petitioner anymore; now I belonged. I spotted the waitress who thought I went to Dickinson. I waved, I wondered how I could gracefully let her know that I had had a big fraternity-type time the night before.

Maybe act a little hung over, ask for some Alka-Seltzer.

I never had a chance. From the moment we got into the booth, Digger took over with a barrage of nonstop hysteria that was incredible even for him.

He started by doing some college cheers ("SISS BOOM BAH"), and then shifted into his own versions, which became progressively strange, disgusting, and obscene.

Then he lit a cigar and announced, "Okay, I'm gonna say it."

"Say what?" Lauren asked in all innocence. I could see the answer slowly dawning on her as she studied the sly grin behind the cigar smoke. "Don't you *dare*," she whispered.

"Yes I am," he said, sitting straight up. "I'm goin' for it."

"You better not."

"Here I go — ffff—"

"*Digger.*"

"Fffffff—"

"*Stop him.*"

Lauren reached across the table at him; he tapped ashes on her hand.

"Fffff-fuh—"

"Let me out!"

"Fuh—"

"Help!"

The waitress arrived. All eyes swung to her, back to Digger. The waitress held her pad and pencil.

"Ready to order?"

Digger drew on the Panatella, blew a bouquet of

smoke into Lauren's face, cleared his throat several times — he had the waitress's full attention — then, delicately, primly, meticulously molding the incomparable syllable, he said *the word.*

The waitress never raised an eyebrow. "Sorry, sir, we're out of that," she replied coolly and took our orders. Wags ordered a pizza steak for a dumbstruck Digger.

Digger didn't stay down long. Pretty soon he had something clever to say every time a waitress went by. He called them all Clara, as in Clara College. ("Hey Clara, where's the next panty raid?" "Hey Clara, I'm the quarterback at P.U.")

The rest of us tried to get some kind of conversation going, but we had to hack every word out of the distracting thicket thrown up by Digger. You had to guard your burger and drink for fear of having them disappear or finding something grisly in them. The more we tried to ignore him, the worse he got.

Suddenly he stopped. Not a peep, not a twitch. Minutes went by. Then I started to notice something. So did the others. Eyes shifted, noses sniffed. I sucked in a long breath through my mouth and held it. Wags rolled back from her place at the end of the table, glaring at Digger. "Neanderthal. Nobody called you Devon."

Lauren slammed down her Coloradoburger and stood up. "I can't eat with that pig around. I'll meet you outside." She started off, wheeled, and came back. She jabbed her finger at Digger. "You know, it's not just *what* you do, which is revolting enough. It's *how* you do it. Even a rattlesnake gives a warning. You're just sneaky. You're" — her eyes spat flame as she scanned her vocabulary; her lip curled as she found the word — "*sinister*." She flung a french fry at him and left.

Digger jumped up, jabbing the french fry after her. "Tellya what, Luscious," he bellowed, "you buy me some wind chimes and I'll hang 'em on my ass!"

The College Grille fell silent. The waitresses — everyone — were staring. Then there was a voice — "Stuff it, duke" — followed by a hollow sound — *donk* — at the precise instant when Digger's head snapped forward and the ash from the Panatella in his mouth jumped into his pizza steak; only then did I see the basketball rebounding nearly to the ceiling and back down into the hands of a scowling, pigtailed girl who occupied the booth behind Digger.

Digger jerked around — "I'll stuff you" — and punched the ball out of her hand.

It's frightening what a loose basketball can do to a restaurant. By the time the pigtailed girl caught up with it — two destroyed booths and a trayful of glasses later — we were dumping money on the table and hauling ourselves — and Digger — outta there.

On the Boardwalk, Digger grabbed my arm and started pulling me along. "C'mon, Rat."

"Where we going?"

"Wildwood. You and me. I gotta get outta here."

I stopped. "Hold it, Dig. I don't know . . . what about the girls?"

"Leave 'em. They're all a pain in the ass anyway."

He lowered his voice. "I know where Mazlo and the guys are staying. At the Sea Horse. It'll be crazy, man. They have beer fights in the hallways, on the balconies. Ocean City sucks, man, Wildwood's *wet.*"

"Damn, Dig, I don't know . . ."

I was fishing around for a good reason not to go, but Digger cut my line. He threw my arm down. "Shit, you don't wanna go."

He stomped off.

"Hey, Dig, I *want* to go. Can't we just take them too?"

When he turned and came back I thought I had changed his mind, but all he did was pluck the Panatella from my pocket, sneer "Mouse," and take off again.

So it was me and the three girls. We toured the Boards (again), checked in on Harvey somebody and his Banjo Boys at the Music Pier (for about seventeen seconds), and finally went to a movie that turned out to be more boring than ol' Harvey.

"I think you should've gone to Wildwood, Rat," commented Wags as we headed for home.

"Then who would protect you defenseless females?"

She swooned. "Ah, such gallantry. A knight in shining underwear. What color weareth we tonight, brave sir?"

"We weareth Chianti."

"Ah yes — Chianti."

As we neared the house, Lauren started forging

ahead, then running up the walk. I could see why: new writing had been added to the note on the door. Lauren looked at it and went on into the house without removing it. Penciled in large letters was the following:

> *Hi Wags,*
> *Stopped by to see you.*
> *See you tomorrow.*
> *Love, RR*

Rocket Rantley.

My gallantry must have gone into remission, because it wasn't long before I was heading up Thirty-second toward the beach. The image of Tennessee in the moonlit dunes still haunted me, although by the time I reached the beach I started to feel a little silly. Did I really expect to find her? Much less, find her in the same spot? Not to mention, did she actually exist?

I turned right at Central, left at Thirty-fourth, and that brought me to the beach, with the patio with the white-and-yellow fringed umbrella three houses to my right, according to my reckoning.

Before me was a spectacular moon-washed panorama of sea and sand and sky, and yet I felt like a back-alley prowler as I hurried along behind the beachfront houses. To my surprise, there it was — the fringed umbrella — right where it was supposed to be. And there were the low dunes and the swale

and the tufted grasses. It was deserted — what else? —
yet so saturated was the scene by my two days of
brooding that it fed back to me a distinctly erotic scent.
My Chiantis began to grow.

All this was instantly erased by a searchlight that
came stuttering up the night. Beach Patrol! I froze,
then knelt, then lay flat on the sand. The motor was
getting louder. The sand was cool on my face. I felt a
small lump under me. I thought it was a stone, but it
turned out to be something in my pocket — the crab
claw that the sea had flipped to me on the jetty. It
smelled faintly fishy. I held it, rubbing it like a charm,
until the sound of the motor was lost in the endless
surf. Then I got out of there quick.

The Fourth Day

Breeze wasn't there. Again.

Every morning I woke up to find only myself and Digger in the room, and it was really starting to bother me. How could anyone be so free, so rootless? It was intimidating, scary even. I couldn't explain to myself exactly why, but I wanted him to sleep in this, our Senior Week house, at least once.

A paint box of colors hung from the white porcelain fixture in the bathroom. Six toothbrush holes — five toothbrushes.

Wags and Lauren were sitting at the kitchen table, sipping orange juice.

I took a seat. "Well, what's for breakfast today?"

"Lauren," said Wags, "you want to pass him the menu?"

Nothing was cooking on the stove. No biscuity breakfast smells. "Where's Timmi?"

"Still sleeping," said Lauren.

After a while of chitchat, during which no one mentioned the Admiral, I got up and boiled some water. Everybody wanted tea. Lauren took cream with hers, Wags took lemon. I took both. When I set my cup on the table, it wasn't looking too good.

"*Gahd,*" Wags gagged, "what did you *do* to it?"

I told her.

She came over, carried the cup off as though it were a dead animal, and made me another, cream only.

Digger came staggering into the kitchen.

Lauren started to get up. "I'm leaving."

Digger pushed her back down. "Don't worry. I never fart before noon." He crumpled into a chair; his head sloshed about. "Where's the grub? Where's Timmi?"

I set some orange juice in front him. "Sleeping."

As Digger came out of his grog, he started regaling us with tales of Wildwood.

He told us about the incredible things you could see — and step in — in the hallways of the Sea Horse Motel.

He told us about this guy who every year gets turned down in his bid for a job at Castle Dracula. He lurks around wearing a black wraparound cape, which he opens in front of selected females. Under the cape he wears nothing but flesh-colored briefs and what appears to be the lopped-off trunk of a large stuffed elephant. The trunk is tied to his waist and hangs down to below his knees; suddenly the guy yanks on a string, and the trunk jumps up and pokes whoever is standing closest. Supposedly some girls of Wildwood consider this a great honor and go looking for the guy, who calls himself "Ejacula."

And he told us about sitting on the front porch of the Sea Horse with Mazlo and the guys, throwing down Buds, when Mazlo says, "Hey, anybody see that?" Everybody followed Mazlo's finger to the motel across the street. In a second-floor window two girls without tops were waving and jumping up and down. Naturally, everybody started whistling. Suddenly two guys came walking across the street. They were bikers, apparently the girls' boyfriends. They looked like gorillas in people suits. One of them held out a tin cup and said if they wanted to see more, there would be a slight charge.

"I'll bet you paid him, too, didn't you?" said Lauren.

"Not me," said Digger, dumping four spoonfuls of sugar into his tea. "I used my credit card."

Digger's tales and more cups of tea filled the time till eleven, when Timmi finally came out. Digger pounded a spoon on the table. "Grub! Grub!" My taste buds ached for pancakes.

But Timmi didn't stop. "Going out," she said, and we all gaped after her as she walked out the front door.

We were down to three — Lauren staying home again — when the beach party hit the road. I went into the water, but with Digger hustling bikinis and Wags basking like a sea otter in ocean too deep for me, I soon got tired of having no one to play with, so I went back to the blanket.

My color was a total disgrace. The first day, of course, wasn't my fault: rain out. On the second day I had proved the perfect guinea pig for Sun Protection Factor 15: it had kept everything — burning rays, tanning rays, pinking rays — away from me. And I had spent all of the third day, thanks to Timmi, under a towel. So the only color I had was on the front half of each foot, marking the end of the towel. I looked as though a medieval torturer had started winching me down into a vat of bright red paint, when the king suddenly burst in and gave me a pardon.

How I envied the bronze bodies lying all around me, bodies with Coppertone built into their very genes. It still made me shudder to think of the day in the summer after ninth grade when I was stupid enough to go to a swimming pool. The instant I stepped from the locker room onto the bright deck of the pool, Mazlo squawked for all the world to hear: "Yo! Look at *this!*" As I chuckled my way good-naturedly toward the sanctuary of the neck-high water, I was the object of more gaping spectators than the geek chomping chicken heads at the fair two miles away. I was cursed. I was a snowman that never melted.

And so I resolved to give it my best shot. No lotion (except over my foot-halves), no towel, just me and the sun, one on one. I lay there and lay there and lay there. I gritted my teeth. I drummed my fingers. I broiled. I roasted. The sun basted me in my own juices like a turkey. I tried so hard to tan I think I grunted. I lay and lay, trying to picture the golden Butterball I was becoming. Then, suddenly, the worst thing of all hit me: I could no longer think! The sun was turning my brain to wax.

I sat up. Sweat poured into my waistband. My head was spinning. I was panting. And I was still white. I looked at my watch — ten minutes had passed.

On the nearest blanket lay a golden girl in a black bikini. She had been there every day. I never saw her go for a dip, or even move. She had no radio, no paperback. Just her and the blanket and the sun. I felt like going over to her and saying, How can you stand it? Aren't you *hot?* Doesn't it drive you crazy, nothing to do but lie there hour after hour? When you're not even tired? What are you thinking about? Anything?

I knew it would be useless to ask. There is a covenant between such bodies and the sun. They are blessed not only with the right skin, but with a total tanning personality that makes them as comfortable in the sun as a hog in mud.

Completely beaten, I picked up my stuff and started for the Boardwalk. Wags was on her stomach on a yellow rubber raft. The head bobbing beside it looked like Rantley's.

I went into a movie. Not for the movie. Or even the air conditioning. I did it for the darkness.

The movie was so bad that I was stacking Z's halfway through it. When I came to, it was after five o'clock.

I went to a drugstore, bought a toothbrush for Breeze, and headed for home. I hoped they hadn't already left for Wildwood.

As it turned out, no chance of that. Digger was fuming around the house, kicking beer cans and wielding a pint bottle of Southern Comfort that he had snatched from Mazlo's room.

"No Wildwood tonight," said Wags. "Car's broke."

A beer can bounced off my shinbone; pain sang to my toes. Another can rattled around the undercarriage of the wheelchair.

Wags steamed for the door. "Let's get outta here."

On the way to the nearest pizza shop, Wags handed me a piece of paper, a note:

Guys,

> *He finally arrived! We're going
> out. See y'all later.*

> *Lauren*

P.S. Don't wait up for me!

"She sounds chipper," I said.

"That's love."

"And Timmi? Where do you think she went?"

Wags just shrugged.

After ordering our pizza, Wags propped her chin on her hands and grinned across the table. "Well,

Mister Umlau, is Senior Week everything you expected it to be?"

I laughed. "Is it *anything* I expected it to be?"

With that, our mouths were off and running. We talked about everything from A to Z — literally. We picked out at least one topic for every letter of the alphabet: "aardvark" (I said it was a bird, Wags said a marsupial) to "zygote."

When we finally stopped jabbering long enough to take a breath, I noticed there were eight crusts on the pizza platter.

"I hate to say it," I said, "but this sure beats the beach."

"Don't hate to say it. Why do you think I stay in the water most of the time?"

"Man, just to talk . . . "

"We were both suffering from C.D.S."

"What's that?"

"Conversation Deficiency Syndrome."

I told her about the golden girl on the neighboring blanket.

She nodded. "I've notice her too."

"Have you ever seen her in the water?"

"Nope."

"Or do anything?"

"Nope."

"How can she stand it?"

"I don't think she has a choice."

"What do you mean?"

She crunched on a crust. "I think she's dead."

Suddenly Wags pushed herself away from the table

and turned to the window. It was getting dark. "Mouse, find Timmi."

I quickly rolled Wags back to the house and set out. I was worried now too. Somehow darkness made a missing girl more missing. Even in America's Greatest *Family* Resort.

I figured I'd take a route that would lead to the Boardwalk, but I never got there. I had only gone a few blocks when I saw someone come wobbling out of a side yard between two houses, cross the street, and disappear into the shadows of another side yard. When he re-emerged, he crossed the street again and vanished between two other houses. That's how he made his way along, stitching the neighborhood together.

By the time I got close enough to confirm that it was Digger, I could hear him muttering to himself. By the next pass, he wobbled by, no more than five feet away, and never noticed me. He was drinking from an orange-juice carton.

I watched him make a few more passes — I couldn't help being amused — before deciding he was pressing his luck and that I'd better grab him. I waited in front of the house where he should have come out next, but he didn't. I kept waiting and he kept not coming.

A high hedge ran along the house from front to back, blocking the moonlight and making a pitch-black corridor. I glanced up and down the deserted street and headed into the blackness. I was near the back of the house, using the peak of a garage roof against the

sky as a guide, whispering, "Digger . . . Digger . . . ,"
when I stepped on something.

"*Ooowwwww!*"

"Digger — that you?" I was fumbling blindly
below.

"Hooz stepp'n on me?" His head came up into
my crotch and kind of bull-tossed me; I came down
all over him. "What th— Help! Mugger! Mugger!"

Light flooded the grass. The silhouette of a person
stood at the nearest window. Somehow I hauled the
both of us out of there and set a course for home.

Digger kept mumbling that he wanted to go back;
I told him fine, because that's what we were doing.

He asked me if it was true that I was going to
college.

"It's true," I told him.

"Which one?"

"You know — Dickinson."

"Dickson?"

"Dick-*in*-son."

"Dick-*in*-son."

"You got it."

"Wherezat?"

"It's in Pennsylvania. Carlisle."

"Far?"

"No, not really. Couple hours' drive."

"When y'go?"

"September."

Suddenly Digger was gone. I looked back; he was
sitting on somebody's front lawn.

I tried to pull him up. He wouldn't budge.

"I ain' gone back."

"Digger, come on. I got to get you back so I can go out looking for Timmi."

"Timmi? Where she?"

"I don't know. That's why I have to look for her. C'mon."

He let me hoist him to his feet.

"Timmi gone too?"

"Yes, I just said."

"College?"

"Nursing school."

"An' Wags gone an' Queenie gone. Ever'body. Even Mazlo" — he dropped onto the nearest grass, wagging his head — "Muh–*reens* . . . Muh–*reens* . . . ever'body *some*place . . . ever'body *knows* . . ."

"Not Breeze," I said. "He dooon't know what he'll be doing the next minute."

He popped up and staggered me with a backhand across the chest. "Breeze doan care, man!" His face was square into mine, his skin flush, his eyes gleaming in the street light. "He doan fuggin' *care*."

"Digger," I said, re-steering him homeward, "if you want to go to college, you can go. Just apply for next year. Maybe the Community College would even take you for this year. September."

We walked in silence for a block or so; then he draped his arm over my shoulders. "Lizz'n, Mouse, here's what we do. We stay 'nother week. Howzat?"

I reminded him that we had to be out of the house before Saturday, that Wags's parents had rented it out for the following week.

His arm tightened around me. "No prob'm. We doan need a place t'sleep."

"I have to get home for my summer job."

The arm tightened; I was inhaling pure Southern Comfort. "Job'll wait. Lizz'n. We get d'car fixt an' we blow it out . . . all day . . . all night . . . tear d'place up . . . show'm how it's done, right, Rat?"

"I don't know, Dig."

"You'n me, Rat."

"We'll see."

He noosed me to a stop. "Right, Rat, right?" He had a Christmas-morning face.

I surrendered. "Right, Digger."

Timmi was back.

Until I saw her, laughing in the kitchen with Wags, I hadn't realized how much I had missed ol' No. 44.

Wags turned, laughing, to face us. Dangling from a cord around her neck was the black cast-iron skillet that Timmi used for cooking.

Wags explained: "As you can see, friends, the prodigal has returned. She has come back to the people who ate her pancakes but knew her not. To the people who left enough dirty dishes to fill a sink, but not enough gratitude to fill a teaspoon. Now, as you can see, I have taken this yoke of guilt" — she rapped the skillet — "upon myself. You needn't go looking for other yokes, I will bear this for all of us. You will, however" — she threw me a towel, Digger a sponge — "do the dishes."

The combination of Digger Binns, Southern Comfort, and a sinkful of suds produced results that gave me and the girls stomachaches from laughing.

At one point, when Timmi left for a minute, Wags tooled over and whispered something to Digger. When Timmi came back, she was greeted by a faceful of suds, followed by five minutes more of Digger's patented persecution. The more abuse he heaped on Timmi, the harder she laughed, and somewhere along the line it dawned on me that until now, Digger had at one time or another picked on everyone but her.

When Lauren came in, she took her faceful of suds without a howl or even a dirty look. She just smiled pleasantly and scooped the suds away.

"My, my," sighed Wags, "those midshipmen sure know how to mellow a lady, don't they?"

"Yo, Luscious" — Digger stepped in front of her — "what's this guy got that I don't, huh? A boat? What else?"

Lauren patted him on the head and smiled. "Class, sonny." She detoured around him, chirped "Ta-ta," and waltzed on back to her room, swinging her shoulder bag.

The moment Lauren closed her door, Timmi leaned in and whispered, "I forgot to tell you. I saw her up on the Boardwalk earlier tonight, and she was with somebody, but" — her voice got even fainter — "I don't think it was Paul."

"Why not?" said Wags.

"I didn't see him real good, but he didn't look

like the guy in the picture. At *all*. He looked older. He had a beard. Fancy shirt. Gold chains hanging over his chest."

"*That*," declared Digger, "was not no Admiral."

Timmi turned to Wags. "What do you think's going on?"

Wags's eyes stayed on the closed door beyond the bathroom. "I don't know. I guess we're not supposed to know."

I was ready to turn out the bedroom light, when I remembered the toothbrush. I found it still in its little white drugstore bag on the TV.

A benevolent voodoo seemed at work as I dropped the bright green handle through the lone empty hole in the fixture, releasing a wishful spirit that swirled about the porcelain and soared off in search of Breeze.

The Fifth Day

Breeze showed up as we were leaving. A red Mustang convertible pulled up to the house, let him out, and took off. The female behind the wheel was not exactly Little Orphan Annie.

"Baccarat dealer," yawned Breeze, moseying past us and up the ramp. "Caesars. 'Night."

A block from the beach Lauren peeled off to go meet the Admiral. I hadn't intended to beach it myself, but Wags had said I should come; we had "business" to do. When we arrived, she pulled out of the blanket a piece of cardboard cut from a box. It was in the shape of a tombstone, and in bold black letters it said:

R. I. P.
HERE LIES A GIRL
WHO DIED
AUGUST 10, 1976
THE REMAINS YOU SEE
HAVE BEEN MUMMIFIED
BY SALT, SAND, AND SUN

I was handed a garden trowel and instructed to dig a hole and install the tombstone just beyond the head of our neighboring blanketeer, which I did.

Then, while the others headed for the water, I started hiking. I figured I'd just keep walking, see if the beach ever did come to an end.

It did, finally, after miles, and I felt a letdown. It was shabby, back-alleyish, not the mecca I had vaguely expected. Its main features were house-high dunes, a jumble of boulders, and a derelict fishing pier.

The massive black boulders, which looked like leftovers of the jetty-maker, were covered with painted messages. One said SHOOBIES GO HOME! The rickety pier was blockaded with barbed wire and a sign saying KEEP OFF THE PIER. Not that anyone would do otherwise. With its tall, thin gray slats collapsing this way and that fifty yards out into the water, it seemed like the burial ground of a race of stilt-walkers. A second sign said SAVE THE PIER.

I climbed a dune and looked back upon miles of beach. If I hadn't known about people, and how they use their seasides, I might have thought I was witnessing a kind of ancient ritual: the white-fringed sea rolling in, forever rolling in, and the creatures coming down to meet it, going into it. I felt kind of wistful for my time back in their midst, when I cozily deluded myself that the beach went on forever; but there's something you can't go back to once you've walked to the end of the beach.

I came down the sandy slope. There was another

sign: KEEP OFF THE DUNES. I wondered if I was a shoobie.

I did not return by way of the beach but the town, a tidy gridwork of cereal-box houses with tidy little blanket-size front yards.

I grabbed a sub and a Slurpee at a 7-Eleven and grazed my leisurely way down Asbury. By now the sun and salt air were having their usual effect on me, and as I turned onto Thirty-second Street I was really looking forward to a little sack time. Then I saw the black Camaro in front of the house, right behind Digger's wreck.

I didn't know which was worse — that Wags was in the house with Rantley, or that now I couldn't go in to take a nap. I walked slowly, hoping Rantley would come popping out before I got there. No such luck.

I was past the house when I heard a voice: "No!" At first it seemed disembodied, a vagrant syllable blown down the empty street from the beach. I kept walking, but I couldn't shrug off the thought that it was Wags's voice. I looked back. The last window on the side was open: Wags's room.

What should I do? I stopped. I didn't go forward, I didn't go back. I did nothing. I just stood there like a moron, pawing at the sidewalk as though looking for a lost dime. Should I go back? Was I imagining things? Was I making a soap opera out of this?

In the end I went back, foolish as I felt, simply because I could not go forward.

I rang the doorbell, my clever strategy being to

say that I hadn't realized the front door was open; plus, this would give them time to get themselves untangled and smooth out their clothes (or even put them back on). But nobody answered the door.

Now what?

I went around to the side. I took about an hour dawdling down toward the back window, feeling sillier every second. In fact, I was right on the verge of switching off "General Seashore" and leaving the scene when Wags's voice came loud and clear through the screened window: "I said no!"

"Wags?" I called.

Silence. Surf-sound like tumbling clouds, faraway storms.

Then a banging of metal, a crash of glass.

"Wags?"

A few seconds later an engine shrieked out front, tires screamed like seagulls.

"I'm all right, Mouse." Wags's voice was lower now, and shaky. "You can come in."

The Camaro was gone. The wheelchair was in the living room. I found her in her room, on the far side of the bed, on the floor, on her stomach, groping with both hands behind her to tie the top of her bathing suit. I knelt. At the touch of my hands hers fell away. I tied the strings as I would a shoelace.

She turned herself over and lay on her back. She was crying.

"Oh Mouse —"

"What happened?"

"I don't know. I was dumb. I thought I could help him. I tried."

She turned her face away, pounded the floor with her fist. One of her legs began to spasm. It rose till the knee was six inches off the floor; the thigh was fluttering.

She reached back; I gave her my hand. She put it on her thigh, rubbed it against herself.

"Knead," she gasped, "like dough, knead, knead."

It felt as though a moth were trapped inside her thigh. I kneaded for a long time. Gradually the fluttering died away. I could feel her whole body relaxing. Her eyes stayed closed. She was breathing easily. She looked asleep. I wondered if I should stop, and wished I would never have to. I kneaded to the rhythm of the sea beyond the window.

In time she sighed and turned languidly back to me. She patted my hand; I stopped.

"What do you mean, you tried?" I said.

She smiled feebly. "I know how you feel about him. You've done a good job of keeping your mouth shut in front of me. I'm not crazy about him either."

"No?"

She laughed. "Not exactly. Never was, really. But I did used to like him pretty much. But then, he used to be more likable. We had some good times. Skiing. Swimming."

She told me the story then, the story no one else knew. About Rantley always badgering her to do it, and her putting him off. And then February, junior

year, ski weekend, Camelback. Even there, high on
the Expert slope, badgering her; and then proposing
a deal — if she made the somersault she was about to
try, he'd lay off her for the rest of the weekend; but
if she didn't make it, that night would be his — and
her saying okay, okay, just to get him off her back.

"Afterwards, for a long while, he stayed away.
Never visited me in the hospital. Then that spring, he
started to come around. One day he mentioned 'the
little deal we had.' I didn't know what he was talking
about. So he reminded me. His face — you should've
seen it — perfectly straight. Serious. I started to laugh.
I didn't know if he was deliberately joking or if he
really expected to collect, but either way it was up-
roarious. Can you see it, Mouse, him there, straight
face, me cracking up?"

I nodded. "I see it."

"Well, as it turned out, I was wrong on both
counts. Turns out, what was bothering him all this
time — why he had stayed away so long — was that
he felt guilty. Responsible. He thought if he hadn't
made me make the deal, I'd be dancing around today.

" 'You're crazy,' I told him. 'Deal or no deal, I
was going to do the somersault. I had been hotdogging
all day. I just said okay to you to stop the nagging.
You didn't *make* me do anything.' So I told him, 'Relax.
Forget it. You're absolved. Who knows, maybe this is
my punishment for lying to you, for saying okay, because really, I would never let going to bed with someone be the price of a messed-up somersault. So clear
your conscience and have a nice day. Good-bye.'

"Didn't see him again till school started. Right away I could see I hadn't satisfied him that day. It got very uncomfortable. For the both of us. Whenever I bumped into him — hallways, lunchroom, wherever — I could see him punishing himself at the sight of me, poor little paralyzed Wags. I wished he would move away, spare himself, spare me, but instead he started to come around again, and by now his guilt was like an elephant on his back."

She took a deep breath, closed her eyes, rested her hand on my foot.

"Took me awhile to figure it out — some of it, anyway — I still don't understand all of it. Seems he didn't believe me when I said it wasn't his fault. He thought — or at least *said* he thought — that I was just being nice, letting him off the hook and all. Sometimes he seemed so miserable, I found myself going to *him*. I cooked up a thousand different arguments to convince him that it was not his fault, that he was only flattering himself, but it was all 'just words,' he'd say.

"And then — like all of a sudden my eyes opened up — and I saw what he was getting at: that there was only one thing that could convince him, that could relieve his guilt. I didn't know if it was true or if it was one of the world's all-time great lines — and I'm still not sure — but whichever, I said forget it, pal.

"But that didn't settle anything. He had started drinking a lot, he got his Camaro, the notches traveled halfway around the head of his tennis racquet. He was making a first-class mess of himself. He even made a scene with me in the gym one day; maybe you heard about it. So what happens? — catch this — *I* start to feel guilty about *him!*"

We both had a head-wagging chuckle over that.

"After all, I had the ultimate power of absolution, right? I was just being too selfish to use it. And anyway, it wasn't as though going to bed with him — one time — would've killed me."

She must have seen something in my face; she started laughing and squeezed my ankle. "I didn't, Mouse. I wouldn't." The laughter left her abruptly; she looked up into my eyes. "Mouse . . . you showed up just in time."

We just looked at each other for a while, and I felt something I had never experienced with Wags before: a sense of equality. It passed quickly enough, but it left behind something else, something that probably could not have turned up without it: a desire for her. *Good God,* I thought, *maybe Wags Hallewagen is destined to be the first one, and not some Tennessee!*

Her hand loosened, fell softly from my ankle.

"So, that's where you came in, so to speak. That's what you were seeing this week, me trying to help, trying to be friends, trying to understand, trying to talk." She pushed herself to a sitting position. "Guess it didn't work, huh? Help me into the bed, Mouse."

She wound up in the bed, so I guess I must have helped, but I sure didn't win any points for style. My long-standing wish to look like Conan — able to lift ladies from floors to beds in one graceful motion — was never stronger than the moment when I let her down and the fall of her weight pulled me like a slung sack onto the bed with her. I shot back to the floor and onto my feet like a cat. She howled.

She held out her arms to me. "Mouse — " I leaned over; she pulled my head down and kissed me. "Thank you. For the second time this week." She gave me a sly, sideways grin. "Are you trying to ingratiate yourself to me?"

I stood up, stiffened. "Madam, I ingratiate myself to no one."

She broke up.

And then she closed her eyes. I hadn't been aware of how exhausted she was. It was time to go.

I paused at the door.

"Wags?"

"Hm?"

"The ocean, the waves, do you, sort of, hear them, y'know?"

She opened one eye, grinned. "Regular chatterboxes, ain't they?"

"Yeah," I laughed. "Sweet dreams."

I closed the door and floated off to my bed.

Digger pummeled me awake with a towel and a bellow: "Wild-*wood!* Wild-*wood!*"

The car was fixed. Wags had called a neighbor, who had come over, cleaned the terminals, and put a charge in the battery.

"I think I need to get out of here as much as Digger," said Wags. She whispered not to say anything about what had happened earlier.

Wags insisted that we wait for Lauren till at least seven o'clock. Lauren opened the door with two minutes to spare. She was immediately surrounded and herded outside. She wrenched free.

"I am not going to Wildwood."

"Lauren," said Wags, "we're all going. We waited for you."

"Well, I don't see Breeze here. Why don't you wait for him?"

"Breeze is around. He's orbiting."

"Well, I'll orbit too."

"Lauren" — Wags nudged her toward the car — "we *want* you to be with us."

"But I'm going back out. Here."

"With Paul?"

Lauren's face reddened. "Yes, with Paul. Of *course.*"

Wags pulled in tight. "Lauren — with *Paul?*"

Lauren just stared at her for a minute, then got into the back seat.

Wags directed Digger to a beer stop at the Point. In Breeze's absence, Digger was sent for the brew. He whipped out his fake ID and came back with four six-packs.

Wags snapped open a can and took a long snort. "Ah — I needed that. On to Wildwood!"

The road followed the shoreline. The ocean was almost never out of sight.

We passed through Strathmere and Sea Isle City

and Townsends Inlet and Avalon and Stone Harbor. North Wildwood would be next. Then Wildwood. I felt for change in my pocket, to pay the bikers. Wags and Timmi were discussing what to do if Ejacula happened to accost them. For Ejacula's sake, I hoped he didn't meet up with Wags. Lauren was fixing her face.

We never got there.

Midway through Stone Harbor the car began to overheat. First the red dashboard light went on, then steam started coming out from under the hood. Pretty soon we looked like a boiling kettle on wheels.

"Hey, uh, Digger," Wags called, "what's going on?"

"No problemo," said Digger. "Little condensation, that's all." He casually lit up a Panatella.

A few seconds later Timmi and Lauren screeched in unison: "Digger!"

Digger still wore a what's-all-the-fuss face. "Huh?"

Lauren grabbed his arm. "We're gonna blow up!"

The hood looked like Vesuvius.

Digger laughed, blowing smoke, "What, *that?* It does that all the time. Waddayou girls know about cars, right, Rat?"

My fingers curled around the door handle.

"Digger," Wags commanded, "stop the car."

Digger stopped smiling. "Soon as we get to Wildwood."

"The only place we're all going is to Heaven if you don't stop this damn car."

"*You* can go to Heaven" — Digger tromped on the gas — "I'm goin' to Wildwood."

"Digger."

Digger didn't answer.

"Digger."

Wags had no effect. Digger's eyes were fixed ahead, his fingers locked around the wheel. The Panatella jutted from his teeth, unpuffed, its neat gray button of ash growing longer and longer as the speedometer needle crept toward 70. The car started to shimmy, and in the smoke and vibration it seemed we must be leaving a launchpad in Cape Canaveral. *Please,* I cringed.

Suddenly, with a muffled bang, the car hiccupped. Green foam appeared and shot back to the windshield. The smell of something burning that was not meant to burn filled the interior.

Digger cursed and guided the retching car to the sandy shoulder. Three of us jumped out and dragged Wags away while the car was still shuddering. We all insisted on toting a share of Wags, so that she flounced along in three pairs of arms like a rag doll. We kept moving away, along a savanna of tall grasses that bordered the road.

Wags cried out: "Digger!"

I ran back. Digger was clenched rigid at the wheel, molded to it. He wouldn't budge. Since the steam was now down to a teakettle wisp, I figured the car was no longer in danger of exploding.

Wags must have figured likewise. "If not Digger, the beer!" she called.

I opened the trunk, got out the wheelchair, unfolded it, set the six-packs on the seat, and returned to the others.

After waiting for a long time for the car to cool down, we made a gruesome discovery: it wouldn't restart. There weren't many cars on the road. The area was pretty deserted — no houses, not even a Mc-Donald's. The road had veered away from the ocean, along what seemed to be a bay. And it was getting dark.

Lauren groaned. "We're stranded."

"Stranded?" echoed Wags, rotating in her chair. "Who's stranded? We have beer. We have the shore. We have each other. That's not stranded — that's a party."

"Well, *I'm* stranded," said Lauren, "and I'm taking the first ride home — back — *some*place." She huffed into the middle of the road, swinging to look in both directions, her shoulder bag flaring like a lavender wing.

A car came out of the dusk, heading south, toward Wildwood. Its headlights went on, then the high beams. Lauren moved to the shoulder, extending her thumb out over the road. The car slowed down. Lauren's face was radiant in the high beams: it was the face she wore in a convertible circling a football field, or under a white wreath of apple blossoms.

The car kept slowing down, but it never stopped. It was packed with guys. As it went by Lauren, several hands reached out and swiped across her chest. The car gunned away, leaving a rally cry behind: "On to the Sea Horse!"

Up the road, Digger slumped and looked after the receding taillights. His arm went up, as if to throw the finger, then slumped back down.

Lauren's face was in her hands.

Wags rolled over to her, touched her arm. "Paul never did come, did he?"

For a long time Lauren didn't move. Then she slowly shook her head.

"Why the big charade?"

Lauren fished a Kleenex from her bag and dabbed her eyes. She shrugged. "I don't know. He told me two weeks ago, over the phone. He met somebody else. A *girl* midshipman."

"Admiralette."

"I couldn't believe it. He dumped me."

"It does happen."

"It was embarrassing. It was disgusting. *Dumped.* I couldn't believe it."

"So you pretended it didn't happen?"

"I knew it happened. I just couldn't believe he wouldn't change his mind. I kept expecting him to show up any minute. I really did."

"When you saw the note — the other writing on it — you thought he had come back."

Lauren nodded, dabbed. "So —" said Wags, "who's the new guy?"

Lauren took out her mirror and started searching for herself in it. "Damn, I can't see. I'm probably smeared all over the place."

Wags turned — "Sorry. Old Miss Busybody here" — and headed back toward us.

Lauren called, "Just somebody I met, that's all."

Wags halted. "High school? College?"

"I don't know. He's a guy."

A full moon was rising through the feathery tops of the tall grasses.

Wags clapped her hands. "Okay, gang, let's see what we got here. Why don't we try going down that path. Will somebody fetch Digger, please."

The path Wags was pointing to was a dirt strip that led through the tall grasses on the other side of the road. As I went for Digger, Lauren kept grousing that she wasn't going down any dirt path to anywhere. Digger was slumped against the car. I opened the beer can that I had shrewdly brought along and waved it under his nose. He didn't even twitch. I took his arm and led him back to the group.

Lauren was holding her ground with her arms folded; Wags was taking a deep breath. "Lauren, listen, you don't have a choice. Who's going to pick us up? All five of us? Somebody in a wheelchair? You saw what happened with those idiots. Forget it. The only way you could get a ride would be alone, and we're not about to let you out here on this road by yourself. So let's just make the best of it. Little adventure, right? Avon Oaks Family Robinson. C'mon. Maybe we'll catch a fish."

Lauren stared at Wags in disbelief. "You're thinking about staying here all *night?*"

Wags shrugged. "I don't know. I wasn't really thinking at all, just goin' with the flow. But yeah" — she beamed an I-just-found-the-cookies face to each of us — "us . . . here . . . all night . . . why not?"

"Fine," snapped Lauren. "I'm walking." She started off toward Wildwood.

Timmi ran after her, grabbed her arm. "Lauren, you can't."

Lauren wrenched away. "I'm going."

Timmi grabbed her again and this time hung on. "Let me go!"

"It's too dangerous."

"I have to go!"

"No."

Lauren sagged and stayed still, emitting squeaks of frustration. Then she pulled Timmi farther down the road from the rest of us and whispered something to her.

"No way!" Timmi blurted and dragged her screeching back to us.

"He wants — that guy wants" . . . Timmi panted — "to take her picture."

"Thanks, Judas," Lauren hissed.

Wags's face blazed as a car roared past. "You have a little appointment with him in his studio?"

"Stop making it sound like that," Lauren sneered. "It's not like that."

"When're you supposed to meet him?"

"Tomorrow morning. Ten o'clock."

"Good enough. We should be back by then. We'll go with you."

Lauren howled. "Don't you think you're getting a little carried away? We graduated, you know. You're not the big editor-boss anymore. You're just another . . . person. And besides, all photographers are not lechers."

Lauren started walking again. I didn't think; I just

grabbed and stopped her. She stomped and screamed. "Stop it! You're not my mother!"

Wags's voice was calm. "Tonight we're all your mother, Laur. We're all each other's mothers."

I was glued to Lauren's back, my hands locked in front of her. I felt really uncomfortable — impertinent — being so close to her, but it was the only way I could hold on as she grunted, squirmed, stomped, and jabbed at me. I had a mouthful of her hair. Then she stopped struggling and lugged the both of us in a semicircle till she was facing Wags. A tremor passed beneath my hands; she was crying.

"Why do you *care?* You don't even *like* me that much."

"That's not true, Lauren. If you're staying at my house this week, you're there because I like you."

"It *is* true. Everybody cheers when I'm the queen of something, and the rest of the time I get ignored."

I heard Wags's wheels crunch over the ground as she approached. "You don't get ignored, Lauren. You just don't get adored, except on Homecomings and May Days. Adoration is for queens, love is for people. It's the Lauren in you we love, not the queen."

I let go. I had to take two good steps back before the longest of the hairs left my mouth.

Lauren came down the path with us. The grass on either side was two feet taller than me. The path was dark. I felt fingers — Timmi's — gripping the back of my jacket.

We came out onto a beach about the size of a

basketball court. It was harder than the one of Ocean City, and a little pebbly. A few faint lights — probably North Wildwood — glowed a couple miles straight ahead along the other side of the bay. To the left, toward the ocean, there was nothing between us and the rising moon.

Wags threw out her arms. "Bee-yoo-tiful!" She cranked herself forward, down to the water's edge. A cloud drifted over the moon, erasing her from view, but her voice came loud and clear: "I name this place Acorn Beach!"

We settled in.

Digger and I went back to the car to get whatever we could. We returned with a blanket, a tarpaulin, two towels, a volleyball, a Frisbee, two ratty bedspreads that were serving as seat covers, and half a pack of Butter Rum Life Savers. The flashlight was dead.

We dumped the stuff off, gave each person a Life Saver, and went back out on a wood-hunting expedition. We headed south along the road.

All this time Digger never said a word. "Dig," I tried, "by the time we're through with Acorn Beach, Wildwood'll look like a Sunday school class."

No answer.

Pretty soon the road took a right turn — smack into a house. And beside the house, a garage. And stacked next to the garage wall — firewood.

Each of us took a log and stuffed as many twigs as possible into pockets and pants. After dumping off the wood, we went back to the car for more kindling.

We struck it rich — glove compartment, ash trays, under the seats, trunk — and returned with overflowing armloads of burnables. Five minutes later a roaring fire was skimming chips of light across the water.

Funny thing: despite the beer, despite having our own private beach, nobody seemed in a mood to party. At least, not in the usual loud and rowdy way. Maybe Digger's mood was affecting us all. But that's not to say we didn't have a good time. We lounged on the tarp and bedspreads and we talked. We talked and laughed and remembered; and as the fire began to dim and soak into the logs, the night seemed to wrap us in a blanket of its own.

"What I wouldn't give for a hot dog and a sharp stick about now," mused Lauren.

"Or a bag of marshmallows," said Timmi.

That's as close as we got to complaining; instead, we got off onto tales of our favorite picnics, and that led to stories about camping out, and that led to stories about Cub Scouts (me) and Indian Princesses (Timmi) and Brownies (Wags) and Mrs. Naylor's School of Baton Artistry (Lauren).

Digger sat on a towel, facing the bay. He didn't contribute any stories, but every fifteen minutes or so the gasp of a beer can opening signaled that he was joining the party in his own way.

So it went: the fire drawing memories out of us as it popped resin balls deeper and deeper into the logs. The only sign of hunger was an occasional crunch signifying that somebody's Life Saver couldn't be hoarded any longer. Basically, beer was what we ate.

We were trading My-Most-Embarrassing-Moment stories when Digger got up and walked off, carrying the last of his six-pack.

"Where to?" called Wags.

"Dippin'," said Digger.

"Skinny?"

Digger didn't answer. He faded into the shadows.

Wags said, "How about singing for us, Timothea?"

I was surprised — that Timmi could sing and, even more, that she started up without a moment's hesitation.

It was strange. It seemed there should be a dial to turn somewhere, or a microphone, or a ticket stub in my pocket. I was uneasy, for myself, for Timmi, for all of us. But Timmi, sitting cross-legged on the blanket, singing to the fire — folk songs — wasn't the least bit self-conscious; neither was Wags, who lay back with a smile and her eyes closed.

Soon I began to relax as well, and as I lay back I began to hear something that the beach blanketeers never hear on their transistors. I heard the music *beneath* the music: one person, one voice, alone, singing in the night, and it was beautiful beyond words.

It was all of this and a song about a horse, a racehorse named Stewball that drank wine but no water, that must have obscured the first sounds from Digger.

"Listen."

Wags was on her elbow.

Then it was clear — screaming, panic:

"Help! Help! Help!"

I was off and running, tripping, falling down, scrambling to my feet, sprinting into the darkness, the screams my beacon.

"Help!"

I plunged into a shallow marsh of knee-high grass, took a sharp left along the waterline and found myself on another beach, much larger than ours. Digger's discarded beer can sat like a silvery exhibit in the moonlight. Then I saw him, backing away from the water, hunched, dropping to his knees.

He was wearing nothing but shorts. His shoulders, his whole body, shook violently; his breath stuttered up and down a stairway; his eyes, fixed ahead, were gorged on moonlight. His clothes were in a pile nearby. I tried to help him get his pants on, but he wouldn't stand up. He kept staring at the water. I could hear sounds — high-pitched tweets, like referees' whistles, as though the wind were carrying across the bay the sounds of a distant basketball game.

Then the girls were coming, Timmi and Lauren both pushing Wags's chair recklessly over the beach, shouting.

"I think he's okay!" I called, draping his jeans as best I could over him.

The girls stopped at a discreet distance. I went to them.

"I don't know, he won't talk. Something in the water, I think."

The word was there, even if no one said it: *sharks*.

Wags pushed off toward the water. We followed. I had never heard of sharks making vocal sounds. As we came near, I could make out another kind of sound, like someone diving from a platform.

"Look," said Lauren.

We froze. She was pointing to her left, to the water's edge. Something was there, something large, long, huge, mounded black, blacker than the night. A sound seemed to be coming from it, a breathing kind of sound — every twenty seconds or so, a quick sipping of air.

We inched toward it. Suddenly it moved, slapping the water and showering us. Lauren screamed and ran. Timmi and I clung to the chair handles.

"What're those noises?" Timmi whispered.

They now sounded less like referees' whistles and more like rusty hinges. Then another splash, farther out.

"There," said Wags. "See?"

Another huge form loomed, this one in the water.

"There!" said Timmi. "And there!"

Lauren returned, wedging herself between Timmi and me, and we just stayed there, turning from one splash, one rusty hinge to another. I started to notice a fishy odor.

"They're all over," Lauren rasped.

The three of us lurched as Wags rolled forward. Turn by turn she moved until she was right up to the one we had first seen. She was looking down at it.

"God in Heaven," she said in a voice that barely reached us. "They're whales."

Headlights raked the living room curtains, followed by a screech of brakes and four quick blasts on a horn. Even so, I didn't believe it was them. The old man, Mr. Dorfman, had said it would take them about an hour to get there, and only a half hour had gone by. Plus, I wasn't ready — the hot chocolate that Mrs. Dorfman had made had just cooled off enough for me to make a dent in it.

Four more blasts, the last a long one.

"I guess it's them," said the old man, squinting out the window. "Musta flew."

Reluctantly, I put down the hot chocolate and got up to go. "Wait, Warren," said Mrs. Dorfman. She scooted away and returned with a plastic carry bag. "This is for you and your friends. Sorry we don't have more young people's food around the house. What are those chips that youngsters like these days? Nachees?"

I accepted the bag, it was heavy. "I think you mean Nachos."

She clapped her hands. "Nachos! That's it. We'll have to stock up on Nachos, Andrew, in case we get visitors again."

More horn blasts.

Mr. Dorfman was holding the door open. A pickup truck was idling outside. I thanked them and left. Mr. Dorfman called: "Say —" I stopped. "Didn't you say you had a fire down there?"

I said yes.

"Well listen, we have a whole cord of firewood — look, over there — stacked on the other side of that garage. Why don't you take a couple logs with you? It's good hardwood. Burns long."

Now the carry bag weighed a ton. I said no thank you and hurried on.

I got into the pickup next to a lady. A man was driving. "Where are they?" he said before I had the door closed.

"Who?"

He glared at me past the lady's nose. "The *whales*. Aren't you the one that saw them?"

"Yeah," I said, "back there."

He shot into the driveway, backed out.

"Around that old junker on the shoulder?"

"Yeah, around there."

The old couple were silhouettes in the doorway, waving, as we laid rubber.

I showed him the path between the tall grasses. I thought we'd get out and walk, but he dropped down a gear and barreled right on — sounded like we were going through a car wash. The night threw its parts at us through the jumping headlights: the silver-shafted grasses, the fire, the bedspreads, a run of bare beach, a gleam of water, the marshy creek, a sharp left turn, more beach, then four kids, one in a wheelchair, scattering from the onrushing beams.

The driver turned the truck to face the water, then backed up to where the tall grasses began. He switched between high beams and low. There was more than one humped form at the water's edge now; they appeared each time the high beams went on. He settled on the highs, left the motor running, and hopped out.

The two of them went down to the water. They both wore high rubber boots and took long strides.

The man had spoken with a kind of twang. I wondered if they were from Texas. The rest of us grouped beside the pickup. Digger was wrapped in the blanket that Timmi had been sitting and singing on. He was still shaking. Lauren had retrieved her shoulder bag from Acorn Beach. I passed around the bag from Mrs. Dorfman. There were apples and cookies.

The couple knelt together at each of the dark forms. Then they waded into the water, diverging as they went. They waded in about waist-deep and stood there. There seemed to be more noises now, of different types. I imagined members of an orchestra trying to tune up with warped instruments. The two then turned back. They came with those long strides unblinking straight up the corridor of headlight.

"You saw them first?"

He was looking at me.

"No, uh — he did."

He turned to Digger.

"When?"

"Huh?" shivered Digger.

"When did you see them?"

"I don't know."

The man drew a whistling breath, glanced at the lady.

"I can tell you what time *I* found *him,*" I volunteered, showing him my watch. "Ten twenty-three." He looked at his watch. I went on: "That probably means he saw them at ten twenty-two, because he started yelling and I took off and it took less than a minute to run from where we were to here. Unless he was kind of in shock and didn't react right away. Do you remember if you started yelling as soon as you saw them, Dig?"

Digger didn't seem to hear. The man was pulling a CB mike from under the dash. He spoke into it for a while, finishing with, "Hell no, don't tell them!" He took the lady back by the tall grass. They whispered. They seemed to be arguing. It reached us as a lot of hissing, with an occasional Yes! or No! thrown in. Finally the man strode back to us.

"Those are pilot whales out there," he said, as though daring us to disagree. "They're stranding. Four have already beached themselves. Looks like more are coming in, might be a dozen, even two. Can't be sure. Anyway" — he turned away toward the water — "they need help."

"How do you help whales?" I asked him.

"Refloat 'em, stop 'em from coming in, anything. They die on the beach."

"So why are they doing it?" Lauren whined. "Isn't it dumb?"

The man turned slowly and stared at her, his eyes like tiny headlights.

"Nobody knows why," came the lady's voice. "There's lots of theories, but it's still a mystery."

"Can we help?" said Wags.

The man hauled buckets and ropes and other stuff out of the pickup and went clanking across the beach. The lady trailed him with her eyes. "We could use you. Volunteers are on the way, but we never had so many come in before. Once we had two at Surf City.

Usually it's just a single seal or dolphin somewhere."

Wags wheeled up to her. "We're from Avon Oaks, in Pennsylvania. This is Digger . . . Timmi . . . Lauren . . . Mouse . . . great names, huh? I'm Wags." She held out her hand.

The lady shook it firmly, laughed. "I'm sorry. I'm Sandy. Hennigan. And that grump down there is my husband, Jim. We're with the Marine Mammal Stranding Center in Brigantine." She snickered. "We *are* the Marine Mammal Stranding Center."

I told her I thought it sounded like an interesting job.

"Interesting?" She shrugged. "Sometimes. Frustrating, always."

"How's that?" I said.

"Tellya what," she said. "You guys start helping out here, and I'll tell you all about it." She lifted rope out of the truck bed. "Did I see blankets back there at your fire?"

"Bedspreads," I told her.

"Well, we can use them. Towels, anything like that."

I think we all snuck a quick glance at the blanket Digger was wearing, but no one said anything. "I'll get them," I said, and took off.

When I got back they were at the water's edge, gathered around one of the whales. I counted five on the beach now. Jim was still with the one at the end, the one that we had seen first. He was dumping buckets of water over it.

Our whale wasn't as big as Jim's, but it was as

long as Rantley's Camaro, and as black. The most strik-
ing thing about it was its head — it domed out above
the mouth, as though the brow had been molded from
a basketball; the effect was kind of Humpty-Dumpty,
I thought. The whale's mouth went halfway around its
rounded face, giving it a perpetual smile — and a perfect fit for a twelve-inch pizza. Even though the mouth
wasn't moving, we heard a "voice" that couldn't have
been coming from anywhere else. It wasn't a referee's
whistle and it wasn't a rusty hinge — it was a piece of
chalk crossing a blackboard at the wrong angle.

Lauren pointed to one of the eyes. "It's crying!"

We all looked. There did seem to be a clear, thick
substance rolling down from the eye, which was set
on the side of the head just beyond the corner of the
smiling mouth. I was surprised at how small the eye
was, and how humanlike in shape.

"Most people would say that's a secretion, because the eye is irritated being out of water," said
Sandy. "And that's true. But who knows — maybe
there's more to it than that. Those sounds you hear" —
she knelt — "are the whales communicating with one
another. They speak as plainly to one another as we
do. Sometimes it sounds like music. For thousands of
years sailors have heard the songs as they go below to
sleep."

She laid her hand on the domed forehead. "These
are very sensitive, very social animals. They follow a
leader — a pilot — that's where their name comes from.
We think" — she nodded toward Jim's whale — "that
big bull there is the leader of this group."

"Blind instinct?" said Wags.

Sandy got to her feet. "Maybe" — she gestured to the thrashing, whistling waters — "that's what it is. But other times there seems to be true intelligence . . . even more . . ."

Wags wheeled forward, reached out and touched the whale. "Caring?"

Sandy nodded. "Could be. The pilot whale is first cousin to the dolphin, and dolphins have been known to push drowning people into shallow water."

I stepped forward and ran my fingers over the whale's skin. It was smooth as glass. Timmi touched too, and then Lauren, a quick, hot-stove fingertip. Digger hung back.

Sandy unfolded a blanket. "Okay now, pay attention. Do not go near the flukes. The flukes are *there* — the end of the tail. In fact, just stay clear of that end of the whale; it can break your leg. Now, take these blankets, bedspreads, whatever, and lay them over each animal — like so —"

The blanket covered about the middle third of the whale.

I asked her why the blankets.

"We'll lay the blankets over the whales and wet them down. That'll help keep the whales cool. Usually the ocean keeps them cool, but when they're exposed to air, which is warmer, their thick coat of blubber is too much, and they start to cook on the inside."

Lauren shuddered aloud.

"This animal," said Sandy, laying another blanket

over the lower part, "is suffering more than we can imagine. Its lungs can't expand because there's solid ground instead of water beneath it. In the water, it floats; here, its internal organs are being crushed by its own weight. Believe me, this creature does not want to be here."

With the toe of her boot she gouged out a hole on either side of the whale, allowing the flippers to dangle. "Flippers are critical," she explained. "If they're propped on the sand, circulation is cut off."

I asked her what else we could do.

"We're going to try to refloat the big one, the leader. If we can get him off, we may be able to turn the ones still in the water."

"How?" I said.

She sort of laughed. "We're not even sure. It's never been done — not successfully, anyway."

She scooped up a bucketful of water and poured it over the blankets. "Okay, let's get working."

Timmi and I each grabbed a pail and a bedspread and started off. Lauren balked. As I walked on I could hear Wags urging Lauren, then Lauren growling, "Okay, gimme a bucket"; and then, about ten seconds later, Wags calling gently, "Lauren, leave your bag with me."

Digger stayed with Wags.

The light from the truck barely reached the whale at the far end. Up close, I could see that it was partly on its side — one of the flippers dangled feebly in the air. Every few seconds its long body flexed and the flukes smacked water that I could not see.

I wondered if I should try to right the whale. To test the idea, I gave a little push with one hand, and promptly learned it would be just as easy to try to move a house.

No sooner had I laid on the bedspread than it came puffing back at me with a basement plumbing kind of gasp — I had laid the spread over the blowhole. I was glad no one was near enough to see what a fool I was making of myself.

I swung well wide of the thrashing flukes to get water. With each bucketful that I poured over the whale, the feeling grew in me that it understood I was trying to help. I sensed its enormity in all ways — in its size, its consciousness, its exhaustion. Humiliation was here: great roamer of the seas, washed up ingloriously at the feet of a 113 pound mammal named Mouse. I felt embarrassed for its helplessness, for its being at my — or anyone's — mercy. I poured with a rising affection all the gallons I had never been big enough to drink.

A bellow rolled up the beach:

"Get her outta here! Outta here!"

Jim was yelling and brandishing something that looked like a spade, and Lauren was racing toward the headlights.

"It's not a fish!" roared Jim. "Tell 'er! It's not a gah-dam *fish!*"

Within seconds we were all huddled around Lauren, who was clamping her ears and sobbing hysterically. Eventually, from gasped syllables, we managed to piece together the story: she had mistakenly poured water down the blowhole of her whale.

We took turns trying to soothe her. I told her about the bedspread blunder I had made.

Sandy took both her hands. "Hey, look, don't pay any attention to him. All you were doing was trying to help. It was my fault. I didn't warn you about that."

Lauren's eyes were wide and wet. "Did I kill it?"

Sandy forced a smile. "No. I'll go make sure for you." She leaned back against the truck and sighed toward the sky. "Listen, guys, before anybody else gets his head bit off, let me say something about that man down there. Jim Hennigan. I met him when I was looking for somebody to teach me how to train seals and sea lions. That's what he used to do. Once. He's always loved the sea, and especially the animals of the sea. That's why he has this job. That's why he works seven days a week. Always on call. Working out of a trailer. Almost no money."

She gazed beyond us, to the water. We were stone silent.

"Try not to get upset if he hollers. He's been to so many of these things, up and down the coast, and most people either treat it like a carnival, or they deal with it in a way he thinks — we think — is wrong. Y'see, Jim's not a scientist. Most of the people in this business are scientists of one sort or another. Their approach is a little different. When a whale beaches itself, they don't always try as hard to save it as Jim thinks they should. They say you can't save a beached whale. They tend to want to inject the animal, and put it out of its misery —"

She scanned each of our faces with mother's eyes.

"— and it *is* misery, like I was telling you. It really is. And the scientists perform autopsies and try to find out why these things happen. But Jim, he would like to try a little harder to save them. He says we're too quick to decide for them how much suffering they can stand. He says sure, they'd like to be relieved of their suffering — who wouldn't? — but not necessarily their lives too." She kept her eyes fixed to a point beyond us, as though the words were being sent to her. "They screwed up and made a wrong turn and wound up on the beach — why should they automatically have to pay for it with a dose of sodium pentobarbital? Let's try to relieve them of their predicament, not their lives."

She took a deep breath, smiled. She reached out and wiped some wetness from Lauren's cheek. "So For a long time he's been almost hoping for this night. If it has to happen, let it happen here, in New Jersey, on *his* beach, where he's got the authority to do it his way. But dreading it too, because he knows we're not really ready yet for a stranding of this many.

"So you see" — she smiled — "deep down he can use you guys. He wants you, even. He's just a little afraid to trust you yet."

Horn blasts came from beyond the tall grass.

"Oops, gotta go. Our volunteers are here. Be right back." Sandy trotted off.

She was back shortly, in the cab of a utility-company truck. The driver pulled up next to the pickup. I helped him and Sandy haul out a double-row bank of lights and fasten them to the roof of the cab. A motor kicked on in the back of the truck; ten saucer-size suns glowed, then blazed a torrent of light that reached across the broad beach and well out into the water. Jim appeared to be digging a trench around the leader whale. Sandy turned off the lights and motor of the pickup.

Pretty soon more vehicles were bouncing across the marshy creek. Other people came on foot. They brought buckets and blankets and ropes and garden spades. One carried a hoe. Almost everyone had a can of Crisco.

Some of the people went down to Jim, others gathered around Sandy. She explained the plan for getting the leader refloated. Jim was already "trenching" it: digging channels all around it — and under it as much as possible — so as to let the water flow in and make the whale easier to move. Then we would try to push the whale out a little and swing it around.

If that worked, it would be time for the "harness." Sandy held it up. It looked pretty simple — a long loop of thick, cloth-covered rope whose ends coupled together. She explained the various features of it. The cloth covering, to prevent cuts and abrasions. (A whale's skin, she said, is more delicate than ours.) The coupling, which could open and close instantly with just two fingers. This could be critical, she said, if the whale started to roll or get into trouble and had to be released quickly from the harness.

Then she picked me to play the role of the whale and draped the harness — a tiny part of it — over me. She showed how it looped over the domed head and down behind both flippers. It might not look like it would work, she said, but it did, because the more the harness was pulled forward, the harder the flippers would clamp down on it. She fitted it under my arms and started pulling me along — she was right.

There was a brief patter of applause, not loud enough for Jim to hear. You could see how proud Sandy was of Jim's invention. And you could see that the caring that went into it was just as enormous as the creature it was designed to save.

Sandy went on to say that once the harness was attached, the whale would be guided into deeper water. At that point, if the whale had been beached for a long while, it might have a hard time floating straight, so people would have to stay with it till it relearned to stabilize itself. Then, finally, a line from a boat would be attached to the harness and the whale would be towed out to deep water and released. If all went well, the other whales still in the water would follow. Hopefully.

"But we can't get started till daybreak," Sandy said. "It's too dangerous at night, trying to bring a boat in with others still out in the water. And by morning the tide will be coming in. That should help." In the meantime, she said, we could trench the other whales and keep them wetted down.

Everyone headed down to the water then, and this time the five of us stayed together. Three more whales had beached themselves. We picked one out and gathered around it. We just stayed like that for a while, each of us, I guess, wondering exactly how to

fit this newcomer into a night that started with Wildwood and beach fire, into a week that began with four
hundred mortarboards sailing into the air. Then Digger took off his blanket and laid it over the whale, and
from that moment on it was "our" whale.

Digger and I did the trenching, being sure to free
the flippers first. Timmi and Lauren poured water.
Wags touched the whale, rubbed, stroked it, even
down dangerously close to the flukes.

The incoming tide, advancing as imperceptibly as
the hour hand on a clock, filled the channels as we
dug them. We had gone a good two feet deep all
around the whale, except for the tail end, when we
heard a voice from a bullhorn. A boat was bobbing
gently in the water some fifty yards offshore. Although
a spotlight beamed like a miner's hat from the top of
the cabin, there was no mistaking the meaning of the
purplish tinge on the horizon beyond: morning had
arrived.

The Sixth Day

Jim, now wearing a wet suit, placed the palms of both hands, fingers spread, against the black domed forehead of the bull whale. Then he backpedaled till his body was nearly parallel to the ground. He gouged footholds from the beach with the toes of his boots. He looked like a sprinter just after the gun has gone off.

Six other men, three on either side, stood knee-deep in the trenches and leaned mightily into the whale.

Jim braced, grunted, "Okay, on three. One. Two. Three."

All seven grunted, heaved, rammed their bodies in unison. They relaxed, looked down. The whale hadn't moved an inch.

"Okay again. One Two. *Three.*"

Again, nothing.

Three more times they tried. The men's faces reddened, and the sky itself seemed to flush with their efforts. Once, the flukes gave a twitch, but the head never budged. I wondered what the whale was communicating to the others.

"Okay, out," snapped Jim. The men climbed panting from the trenches.

Jim grabbed his spade and with the long, broomstick-like handle began scraping at the submerged sand beneath the whale. After ten minutes of furious action, during which the rest of us watched silently, afraid, I think, to move, he dropped the spade, leaned gasping into the domed head, and nodded. The six men jumped instantly into the trenches.

"One. Two. Three."

Someone in the crowd squeaked; the soles of Jim's boots stood at right angles to the beach: movement!

"Again!"

The men grunted and heaved —

"Again!"

— sloshed and slipped in the trenches as the huge blubbered bulk inched along. All of a sudden one of the men yelped and lurched into the whale; he pushed himself out of the trench and lay on his back, clutching his knee and swearing.

"Somebody — jump in!" Jim commanded, and before I had time to think about it there I was, wedged between two men twice my size, helping to push a whale out to sea.

"Again! . . . Again! . . . Again! . . ."

I put everything I had into it. My shoulders, my chest, my cheek snuggled against the cool, smooth, rubbery skin. We kept knocking each other's feet, stumbling, but we heaved to Jim's commands like oarsmen in an ancient galley. Against my pressed ear the whale's breathing sounded like one of those old steam locomotives chugging to make it up a hill.

Little by little the water was getting deeper, and the whale was getting lighter. When the water got to be waist-high on me (thigh-high on the others), Jim called, "Okay — hold it, hold it."

Sandy gave him the harness. He worked it over the whale's head, behind the flippers, just as Sandy had shown us. I reached beneath the water and felt the tension of the flipper clamping down on the harness.

"Stand clear," said Jim.

As we moved back, he swung the whale around, very slowly, till it was facing seaward. And that's when the whale started to list; a flipper poked out of the water, a corner of the smiling mouth rode up.

"Hold 'im!" barked Jim. "Stabilize!"

We rushed in and righted the whale. Then it started to sink, and suddenly we were trying to hold it up on six shoulders.

"Sandy! Floats!"

A huge pair of pink floats, twice the size of basketballs, came flying and plopping into the water. Jim handed each float to someone on either side, then dove under the whale, holding the strap that joined them. In a moment the whale was rising from our sagging shoulders, buoyed by its new water wings.

"He's not ready," said Jim. "We'll have to coax him back. We'll only need a couple for this."

"I'll stay," I said.

Jim looked at me, as though noticing me for the first time, but he said nothing. So it was me and Jim and another man, with a red beard. We introduced ourselves and shook hands over the back of the whale. His name was Shawn. He wore a wet suit too; I was the only one without one.

With Jim tugging gently on the harness, we steered the whale in a circle. Jim said that even with the floats, the flukes were dragging on the bottom. He told us to stay close to the whale, to rub its skin and try to let it know that pretty soon everything would be okay and it would be out to sea again and heading north for some of that great Nantucket squid.

Jim just kept on, and it soon became clear that it was the whale he was talking to, not us. Over and over he described the "scrumptious squid" and the "mouth-watering mackerel" and the "home-style herring" waiting in the North Atlantic cafeteria, and as I shivered and walked on tiptoes to keep my chin above water when the circle made its outer arc, my stomach ached for a steaming seafood dinner.

As we went round and round, we seemed to be cranking the sun into view. The spotlight on the boat went out, then the bank atop the utility truck. The day was on its own.

Every so often Jim would hand the harness to Shawn and go "aft" to massage the stock, which is the main tail part before the flukes. Once, as he was leaning into the stock, it came up, not fast, but enough to send him sprawling backward into the water. He came up sputtering and laughing. "Hey, now we're getting somewhere. Howdja like to arm wrestle, ya fat guppy?"

Most of the time I was absorbed with what I was doing, and listening to Jim's monologues. There were moments, however, when the whole scene appeared before me with an unreality to match any dream: me, taking a whale for a walk; other whales meandering and whistling and breaking water in ways that seemed more like recreation than anything else; and on the beach, an assortment of people somberly digging trenches around and pouring water on still more whales.

"You okay?"

Jim was staring at me.

"Yeah, no problem."

The sun was clear of the horizon, float-pink.

"Okay," said Jim, "let's try 'er again."

He removed the floats and flung them toward the shore; for an instant there were three suns in the sky. The whale dropped slightly, then held, only the dorsal fin and top of the back and domed head above water. It was floating. I heard something like cheering, but it seemed to come from across the universe. My only world now was one whale and water so high to my eyes that it kept lapping over the sun.

Jim, wading backward, huddled close to the head, speaking softly. I too, somehow, with my hands, my will, tried to reach the will of the whale. Once, reaching down, I felt for the flipper and stroked it, and for a few seconds the flipper closed and held my hand against the body.

Jim straightened up. "Decision time. He's not

getting a whole lot better, and I don't think he's gonna get a whole lot better right here. We'll start towin'."

He waved and yelled to the boat. The motor revved; the boat began to creep forward. That's when I felt it — a shudder moving through the whale; then, instead of the usual long-winded exhalations, the blowhole gave a few short gasps, and then nothing, silence. The whale rolled on it side, and for a moment its eye was right there, inches from my own, and I saw my face gaping in horror, then washed from view as the whale began to sink. Crazily, I tried to shoulder it back up. I had the notion that if we could just buy a little time, Jim would come up with a way to give it artificial respiration. But the huge body was sinking like a sofa, and I was going with it, under it, its bulk a dark thundercloud above me, my heels scraping the bottom, and then, as it continued to lazily roll, I discovered that the underside of a pilot whale is not black but pale and creamy. Then a strong hand had me by the wrist, pulling me out, up, but something wasn't coming — the dead whale was lying on my feet. Panic — and then suddenly I was yanked free, popping to the surface and gasping for air.

Half dragged by Jim, I staggered out of the water and collapsed onto the beach between two whales. I let out a string of belches that any college senior would be proud of; it felt like I had just chugged a half-keg. My friends were kneeling around me, all eyes.

"Okay, Mouse?" Wags asked me, but I could only nod as I went on belching.

Digger cracked, "You barbarian. Say excuse me."

I tried to smile. It was good to see Digger getting back to his old self.

Then Sandy was leading me to her pickup and shutting me in the cab with a towel and some dry clothes. I dried off and changed — I was glad I had worn my plain old white Fruit of the Loomies — doing my best to keep below the dashboard. The shirt was a red-and-black lumberjack plaid; the pants were baggy and gray and paint-splattered. It took me forever to roll everything up so my hands and feet would stick out. When I stepped down from the cab, my so-called friends beached themselves laughing.

Sandy steered me to a nearby van, where she brought me hot tea and doughnuts. She watched me till I finished, then she took my cup and said, "Now, get some rest."

"I'm okay," I told her.

She just pointed to the rug-covered floor of the van and closed the door.

In no time I was back out on the beach. I got there just in time to see Jim, who now looked like Paul Bunyan, rising out of the bay, shedding water, leaning into a great rope, and hauling the leader up and onto the beach. He straddled the whale and began to press deeply, methodically, into its back, and each time he pressed, a gob of water spilled out of the blowhole. As he pressed he leaned down and talked to the whale and kissed it. He looked like a cowboy. Then the whale blinked, a flipper twitched, and a great geyser of water shot triumphantly from the blowhole. Jim waved his hat. "He's alive!" The crowd cheered wildly, and the whale, as if to punctuate its joy, began thumping its flukes on the beach. Its exuberance was contagious; soon we all were thumping our feet, matching the rhythm of the happy whale . . . thump-thump-thump-thump-thump . . . *faster, louder . . .*

Thumpthumpthumpthumpthumpthumpthump

The walls of the van came into focus as I woke up. I opened the back door and leaned out. A helicopter was passing directly overhead, low; I could see the pilot. There were big letters on the side — it was from a TV station. The copter curled twice around the sky and thumped on out of sight.

I sat on the edge of the van, my eyes aching from the light. There was no joy — the leader was dead. A pink buoy bobbed in the water where the leader had gone down. More whales had beached; eleven altogether now. Some people were manning buckets, others were in the water, mingling with whales still afloat. A pair of boats dawdled beyond. Gulls swooped in, screaming; they seemed to be having a dialogue with the whistling whales. There were no human voices.

I let myself gingerly to the ground; even so, my legs almost gave way. One wobbly step at a time, I moved forward.

Somebody had my arm, shaking it. Wags. "Mouse, you jerk, you're sleepwalking. Get back there in that van."

"I'm awake," I told her. "Light's bothering my eyes, that's all."

Timmi came rushing. "Hacksaw's here!"

"Oh no," groaned Wags.

"Who's Hacksaw?" I said.

"Hacksaw's a guy from the government, Fisheries something. Sandy says he's the worst one when it comes to putting them out of their misery. He wants to euthanize them the second they hit the beach."

"He's always got a needle and a hacksaw with him," said Timmi.

I asked them why the hacksaw.

Timmi winced, looked to Wags.

"They do autopsies on the dead ones," said Wags. "One of the things they check on is the whale's age. They can tell that from the teeth. But the teeth are so hard to get out, it's easier just to lop off the whole lower jaw. That's where the hacksaw comes in." She turned to Timmi. "Where is he?"

Timmi pointed. "There, talking to Sandy."

The man wore a lemon-yellow windbreaker and a red baseball cap; it seemed he should be all in black. He carried a small suitcase.

Wags took my hand. "Mouse, that was . . . really good, you out there. You really tried."

"Yeah," I said, "and the whale really died."

"They almost always do, Sandy says. Actually, not even almost, but always. There's never been one that lived after landing on the beach."

"Never?"

"Not that she knows of."

"So what was the use?"

"Well, like Sandy said, trying, giving him a chance to lead others back out. Jim hates the needle, even when he knows there's no choice."

"That's why we're trying to keep the others from coming in," said Timmi. "Sometimes you can turn them back if they're still in the water" — she looked at Wags — "didn't she say?"

"Sometimes," said Wags.

I scanned the black bodies up and down the beach. "And these?"

Wags's eyes swung toward the brightly colored man with the suitcase. "All we can do is try to help them suffer a little less."

Jim's voice boomed across the water: "Go! Get outta here! Don't let me see your ugly face around here again! Ever!"

He shook his fist at a boat that was pulling slowly away. Ten yards behind the boat, linked by a rope straight as a pointer, was the humped, finned form of a pilot whale.

I spent the rest of the time there at the water's edge, with Wags and the beached whales. Most of the other volunteers had been deputized by Jim to help with the ones in the water.

We gradually became a team. I would keep the blankets wet while Wags smeared Crisco on the uncovered parts, especially the head and flippers. Sandy had said that a whale's skin could blister before your eyes in the hot sun. I wondered if 15 was a high enough Sun Protection Factor for a whale. Someone came along pouring crushed ice over flippers, but there was only enough ice for one flipper per whale.

For whales just coming in, we had to start at the beginning. First a blanket, wetted by dipping directly into the water; then we dug holes for the flippers, Wags spading from her chair on one side, me on the other. It was like a perverse assembly line: every time a cheer went up because another whale was on its way out to sea, we would turn to find we had a new arrival on the beach.

The time came when a whale arrived and no blankets were left. We discussed what to do. We decided to see if we could find a whale that had died, and if so, take its blanket. After a walk up and down the beach that made the both of us feel ghoulish, we agreed on one. It hadn't made the slightest sound or movement in five minutes, and its eyes were looking a little cloudy. Two flies danced around the blowhole.

I knelt and stared at it, face to face. I touched it. Nothing. I slipped the blanket off. We had just turned away when we heard behind us the unmistakable sound of a blowhole exhausting. The flies were gone. I frantically threw the blanket back over the whale, and never again — gratefully — did we attempt to pronounce death.

From then on we alternated blankets, making sure that every whale was covered most of the time. This meant that bucketing was more important than ever, because the uncovered whales needed a constantly replenished "blanket" of water. And even now, months later, September at Dickinson, whenever I lift something heavy — especially if by a handle — the ache in my shoulders and arms takes me back to that day, and I am once again — as if I have never stopped — hauling bucketfuls of water from the bay.

The flashbacks happen a lot:

Timmi drags herself from the water, slumps to her knees.

"They're coming back."

"What do you mean?" I ask her.

"They're restranding themselves. They tow them out and as soon as they let them go they head back. That first one . . . on a beach a mile from here." She looks up at Wags, almost pleading. "Why?"

Wags cannot answer . . .

I think I'm seeing things. At the far end of the beach, near the marshy creek, a little boy sits on the head of a whale while a grown-up backs away, peering through a camera . . .

The sky is full of screaming gulls.

"Beach buzzards," sneers Wags . . .

A shriek. It's Lauren, waist-deep in water, her eyes bulging, her mouth wrenched and distorted, holding something in her hands, reddish, messy. Sandy reaches her, leads her to the shore. It's a baby whale, stillborn, practically into Lauren's hands. It's about three feet long.

Several things strike me about Lauren. She does not try to give the calf to Sandy, and she does not throw it down when she reaches the beach. Instead, she kneels and lays it gently in the sand, next to one of the beached adults. Also, Lauren is a total mess. Her makeup is gone. She looks like everyone else: a drowned rat. She doesn't seem to notice, or care. She heads back into the water. She is missing her appointment with the "photographer" . . .

Someone brings food. A sandwich, a half-pint of orange drink.

A crab the size of my thumbnail scuttles into a blowhole. I can't eat . . .

Digger and someone in a wet suit carry a canvas stretcher from the water. On the stretcher lies a whale. It is bigger than the stillborn, shorter than the length of the army-green canvas. The stretcher is laid in the bed of the pickup, and the pickup is driven off. Digger stays with the stretcher . . .

Tug o' war:
Jim, wild with exhaustion and frustration, is grabbing a nearly beached whale by the flukes and shouting No! and trying to pull it back out . . .

Timmi tending a humped form in the water, as she might a cradle, singing "Stewball" to it . . .

The man in the lemon-yellow windbreaker is opening his suitcase . . .

The whales are crying.

The sun was behind the beach, propped on the tall grasses, when we realized once and for all that it was over. Mechanically, half-asleep, we had been working our way along the line of whales. When we got to the last one, we turned and saw Hacksaw two bodies away, filling a six-inch hypodermic needle from a dark brown bottle.

"Is it right?" I said to Wags. "Is it really the humane thing?"

She shrugged and gazed sadly at the whale. "I don't know. I wish to God we could ask *them* how *they* feel about it."

We stayed with the last whale until the men approached. With my last reserve of strength, I pushed Wags across the beach. Our shadows were longer than ourselves.

The Seventh Day

My first thought, upon waking, was *When did I get these pajamas?* Then I remembered: the lumberjack plaid. One of the mile-long sleeves had unrolled, so that I now appeared to have no right hand. I still wore the baggy, paint-splattered pants.

My watch was still on my wrist. It was almost noon.

The person sleeping in the other bed was not Digger. It was Breeze.

I remembered getting into someone's car, and Sandy telling the driver where to take us. I remembered bumping across the beach, slashing through the jungle of tall grass. Then people, crowds. We had had to go slowly while they parted. Flashbulbs had gone off.

I tried to sit up but only made it halfway before flopping back down. I felt as though I had just done a thousand pushups. Not that the middle of my body hurt — it didn't even seem to be there. From belly button to spine, I seemed to be nothing more than an empty sausage casing.

I pushed myself up, finally making it to a sitting position on the edge of the bed, and in the process discovered that blinking was the only thing I could do without pain. When I tried to stand, all the pain constricted in a thong around my right ankle. It was swollen and bruised. It took me five minutes to reach the door.

The girls were in the kitchen. They applauded when I hobbled in.

I plopped into a chair. "Man. I can hardly walk."

Wags winked. "I know what you mean."

I wanted to crawl into the saltshaker.

Wags rolled over, pulled me to her, and nearly sucked my cheek off with a loud, squeaking, one-minute smooch: ". . . Mmm-*ah!* Sorry, Mouse, my twisted sense of humor. Say" — she backed up, looked me over — "you're really setting new standards in men's fashions this week, aren't you?"

"Think I'll grow into them?"

She tweaked my cheek. "I think you already have, big boy."

"We brought your other clothes back," said Timmi, pouring me some orange juice. "I washed them. They're in the dryer now."

"Along with all your other clothes," twinkled Wags. "We just couldn't wait to get our mitts on those new undies of yours."

"That's the last you'll see of them," I said. "My

modeling career's over." They groaned. "Say, where's Digger?"

"Still at Jim and Sandy's," said Wags. "I called earlier."

"The one they took in the stretcher?"

"Still alive. Digger's helping them with it."

Lauren — still without makeup, yet beautiful in a totally different way — lifted a newspaper from the countertop and set it in front of me. The headline said:

29 Whales Strand at Nelson's Cove

Under that was a picture of Wags and me tending to a whale.

I winced. "Twenty nine. Jesus."

"Twenty-four, though, really," said Lauren. "The calf was saved, and four others were towed out to sea."

"Deduct two," said Wags. Sandy said two of them restranded overnight at Townsends Inlet."

Lauren, who was washing dishes, slammed down the dishrag, splashing water onto the floor. "God, what's the use?" She picked up a towel and started drying a saucer, round and round. She kept her face to the wall; her voice creaked. "I mean, if they want to die *that* bad. Who are we to stop them? Why save something that doesn't *want* to be saved? Maybe it's the way things are. How do we know? Maybe we're meddlers. Maybe we should mind our own business. Probably been stranding themselves in peace for millions of years, before we had to come along. Look at the lemmings. Nobody's rushing out to save them. They want to jump off cliffs, let them jump off cliffs. So why go getting all upset about whales? What's the difference, huh? What's a whale to us?"

Her voice stopped there, though she continued to dry the saucer. No one answered her questions.

I was back in my own clothes, sponging the bathtub — my bedroom and the bathroom were my parts of the house to clean — when I heard the front door slam shut. I looked out the window and saw Breeze heading up the street. He wore sneakers, his bathing suit, and an unbuttoned shirt. A towel was draped over his neck, and slung over one shoulder was a pillowcase, its contents too meager to deserve the word "bulge." His stride, as always, was bouncy, jaunty.

I grabbed the bright green toothbrush and hobbled through the house. The living room was lemony — Timmi was Pledging the coffee table.

"He's going?" I said. "For good?"

She shrugged. "I guess."

"Damn. Twelve years and no good-bye?"

I hurried into the dazzling sunlight, but something halted me at the sidewalk. I raised my arm, I was about to shout — I couldn't. I shaded my eyes with the wet sponge and just watched him go. I was sure I would never see him again, unless someday I happened to be strolling the right beach of Singapore or Bali or Montego Bay. There would be many hellos for Breeze, but few good-byes. There was no telling where he would wash ashore next, but there was not, I was certain, a beach in the world that he could not get up and walk away from.

I tossed the bright green toothbrush into the kitchen trash can. It plinked off the glass of the Admiral's picture.

We were all packed, including Digger's stuff, waiting in the living room for Digger's car. Sandy had called to say someone would go out and try to get it started. If it started, the person would bring the car to us, and then we could drive to Brigantine to pick up Digger.

The car would not arrive till after five, we were told. We debated what to do in the meantime. We considered checking out the beach for a final time. Or a last lap of the Boardwalk. Or the College Grille. Or going for a pizza. We just hemmed and hawed a lot, until Timmi said, "Who knows, maybe the car'll get here *before* five." That ended all debate. No one said anything directly, but it was clear that the only place we all wanted to go was home.

"Well," said Wags, "I guess this is as good a time as any —" She reached into her suitcase and pulled out three boxes. They were wrapped with newspaper and Scotch tape. "Little mementos of Senior Week. I should get a medal for the trouble I went through to get this stuff without you guys knowing. Timothea?"

Timmi unwrapped hers. It was one of those little ivory-looking statuettes of a dumpy-adorable lady and the inscription WORLD'S GREATEST MOTHER.

Out of Lauren's flat box came a framed picture.
The frame was fancy, gold-colored filigree — fit for a
queen's portrait — and the picture itself was a snap-
shot of Lauren, obviously taken by Wags the night
before with Digger's OneStep — a most unqueenly
Lauren Parmentier, sprawled across her bed, conked
out, mouth agape, dirty and wet and stringy and bloody.
She couldn't take her eyes off it.

"Notice anything missing lately?" Wags said slyly,
handing the third box to me.

I tried to think, and it came to me an instant
before I opened the box: the crab claw! It was now
satiny with plastic coating, and it was dangling from a
silver chain.

No one could speak.

Wags took the crab pendant from me. "Here."
She held it open; I slipped into it. "Remember me
down in Dickinson."

"Man," choked Timmi, "we *are* going to keep in
touch, aren't we?"

A man pulled up in Digger's car at exactly 6:14.
He was basketball-tall to start with, and his greasy,
brown overalls were so long it looked as though his
legs went up to his neck.

He waved a grimy metal disc in front of me.
"Thermostat. Shot. I put a new one in. Gaveya some
gas. Quarta oil. Antifreeze —" He squinted down at
me, measuring. "You Mouse?"

I nodded.

He dangled the keys, dropped them into my hand. "Not your car, is it?"

"No," I said.

He wagged his head and gave a faint, creaky whistle, and for an instant I heard the whales again. "Piece-a work. Oh — brake fluid too. Well, thereya go. Hope it gets you home." He squeezed my arm, smiled sincerely at me and the girls, who were bringing the luggage outside. "Good job yesterday. Good try."

He got into a car that had followed him and was gone.

At 6:19 we were on our way, me driving. I tried to pull the front seat up, but of course it was broken. I had to work the pedals with my toes.

We headed down Thirty-second Street to Central, Central to Fifteenth, Fifteenth to Ocean — past the people heading home from the beach (Would a girl named Tennessee be waiting in the dunes that night? I guessed I'd never know. But then, it didn't seem to matter much anymore), past the back of the College Grille, past Ninth Street, past the amusement park at the end of the Boardwalk, the slowly turning galaxy of the Ferris wheel, the last of Ocean City looming in the rearview mirror.

I followed Brigantine Avenue, as Sandy had directed, till a lighthouse appeared in front of us.

"There it is, Mouse, left," called Timmi.

There didn't seem to be a parking lot, or even a driveway. I pulled onto the dirt shoulder in front of a high chain-link fence. Behind the fence were a trailer and a low-slung building that looked something like a garage, only longer. A sign on the green plaster wall said:

MARINE MAMMAL

STRANDING CENTER

Sandy came out and showed us a gate to enter. She was grinning and holding her finger to her lips. She motioned for us to follow.

She led us behind the low-slung building, where a rutted, pebbly beach tapered down to the bay and a small, gray, weather-beaten dock. Sandy led us tip-toeing over an elevated, rickety walkway. Erected along some thirty feet of the water's edge, forming a "T" just before the walkway broadened into the dock, was a wooden wall of planks that looked a lot newer than the rest of the structure. Sandy stopped and grouped us at that point, then motioned for us to move quickly to the edge of the dock.

When we did, we found ourselves looking at a kind of slapdash pool within the bay. The left and right sides were formed by chain-link fencing; the far side appeared to be the sunken rusty hull of an old boat; the fourth side was the wooden wall we had just crossed over. And directly below us was a sight that I know none of us will ever forget. Digger, wearing a wet suit, was lying on his back, mostly in the water, only his head resting on the dry beach; lying on top of Digger was the rescued calf, its chin resting on Digger's chest. Digger's arms were folded loosely around the young whale, and on his face — was it my imagination? — was an expression I had never seen there before: serenity. If his eyes had been open, he would have been looking straight up at us.

No one spoke. No one moved.

After a while Sandy herded us back down the walkway and up to the trailer.

"I'll wake him up in about an hour," she said. "Even with the wet suit you can't take more than three hours of that water."

"Sandy," said Wags, "isn't Digger coming home?"

Sandy looked sheepish. "I guess not. Not yet, anyway. He told me to tell you to take his car."

Then she filled in the story. From the time they had loaded the calf into the pickup truck, Digger had never left its side. She said pilot whales can't stand being alone. They need company, it's as simple as that. And if there are no other whales around, a person will do. And an unweaned baby such as this one not only needs company, but a mother to take care of it.

"Ideally," she said, "somebody ought to be in the water with it twenty-four hours a day. Between Jim and myself and some kids we can call on from around here, we had plans to come as close to that as possible, but he keeps telling us, 'Don't call anybody, I'll take care of it.'

"The calf isn't doing too good," she said. "Won't take formula. Just lying there in the shallows. I noticed what the sand was doing to its underside, chafing it raw. Next time I looked, there were the two of them, like that."

She reached into the trailer and pulled out a pinkish rubber bag with a flexible tube leading from it. It looked like the enema contraption I've seen in our linen closet at home. "Here's the baby's bottle, if we can get it to feed."

She asked us if we'd like some iced tea; we said we had to get going.

Sandy walked us out to the car. Unlike some people, she didn't start whistling and looking the other way as we helped Wags out of the chair and into the back seat.

"So, where will Digger stay?" asked Wags. "Besides out there?"

"With us. Jim's already starting to like him. I can tell. And you guys too — all of you — he really appreciates what you did. He'd tell you himself but he has to be back out there, seeing to the burials."

"Oh, the others," piped Lauren. "Two of them? They made it?"

Sandy dug her hands into the pockets of her jeans and shook her head. "Fisherman found them. In a tidal marsh near Strathmere. This afternoon."

Lauren slumped back. "One left."

"I hope so," said Sandy. She leaned into the car, almost whispering. "I didn't say anything to him — Digger — but unweaned whales from strandings don't usually last more than a week or two. I don't think any have been known to survive."

"Well," said Wags, "I think maybe this one's got a chance. There might be one whale there, but there's two survivors."

Sandy just kind of blinked at Wags, the way I've often seen adults do. Like, Did *that* just come out of the mouth of a *kid?*

Wags handed Sandy a newspaper-wrapped box. "Give this to him. From his fellow Senior Weekers."

Sandy took the box, waved, and we pulled away.

"What'd you give Digger?" asked Lauren.

Wags hesitated. I could see in the mirror that she had hoped somebody would ask.

"Wind chimes," she grinned.

One clattering car, four howling graduates.

We followed red-and-blue signs to the Atlantic City Expressway. As soon as we got onto it, I pulled off to the side and stopped. I didn't say anything. I turned off the motor, took the keys, went to the trunk, opened it, took out two blankets and some towels, draped them over the back of the driver's seat, and when I sat back down — *voila!* — my feet were flat on the pedals.

Back on the road.

Was it possible? Was that me, exactly one week ago, whipping my mortarboard into the sky? I felt as though I were returning from across the universe. From another time. The sun was setting straight ahead. In the west. Over Pennsylvania.